BLESS
EWE

BLESS
EWE

More Stories for All Seasons

by Jeff Kunkel

FACE TO FACE BOOKS

FACE TO FACE BOOKS is a national imprint of Midwest Traditions, Inc., a nonprofit organization working to help preserve a sense of place and tradition in American life.

For a catalog of books, write:
Midwest Traditions / Face to Face Books
3710 N. Morris Blvd.
Shorewood, Wisconsin 53211 USA
or call 1-800-736-9189

Bless Ewe
© 2000, Jeff Kunkel

Cover design by MacLean & Tuminelly, Minneapolis.
Cover artwork is from an original watercolor painting, titled "Sheep in Winter Morning Light," © 1991, by Steven R. Kozar. Courtesy of Wild Wings, Inc., Lake City, Minnesota 55041.

Library of Congress Cataloging-in-Publication Data
Kunkel, Jeff, 1954-
    Bless ewe : more stories for all seasons / by Jeff Kunkel. – 1st hardcover ed.
        p. cm.
    ISBN 1-883953-31-6 (alk. paper)
        1. Christian fiction, American. 2. Wisconsin – Social life and customs – Fiction. I. Title.

PS3561.U53 B57 2000
813'.54 – dc21
                                        00-032928

First Hardcover Edition

for Anali, Maria,
and Leticia

Acknowledgements

The stories in this collection have been inspired, shaped, and strengthened by many people.

I especially wish to thank those individuals who have told me about their experiences in such a way as to allow me to write beyond my direct knowledge. Donna Thorp told me what it was like to grow up next door to a giant. Edna Mitchell told me what it was like to be a woman laborer in an American steel mill during World War II. David Huck told me about Walter Winchell, one of America's most famous radio commentators. Rick Abrams, Jack Godden, Jay Martin, and author Paul Creviere, Jr. taught me about the life of a 19th-century Great Lakes schooner captain.

I also want to thank those who have helped me prepare these stories for publication: Paul Hessert; Pamela Gullard; Mary Elyn Bahlert; the members of my writing group – Joe Anastasi, Sandy Bails, Ron Parker, and Sally Small; and my editor, Phil Martin.

Special thanks are due to those who have listened to me read my stories aloud. A live audience, responding with arms, legs, faces, groans and laughter, gives a writer much to consider!

Finally, I thank those in my extended family – uncles, aunts, grandparents, and cousins – who told and cherished stories in front of children like me. If it's quiet, I can still hear their voices and see their faces.

THE STORIES

STONE FENCES

OSCAR AND MATTIE SAT at their kitchen chairs, his left knee touching her right knee under the table. Oscar looked out the window at his orange tractor, which sat on top of dark, freshly turned earth. "Tractor plowing ain't all it's cracked up to be," he said. "Maybe I ought to go back to horses."

Mattie, sorting the morning mail on her lap, spoke without looking up. "When you plowed with horses, you complained about them. Couldn't wait to get that tractor, as I recall."

"When I plowed with horses I could hear the birds sing and smell the fresh ground. Now I hear engine chug and smell engine stink."

"Oh!" Mattie said, her face lifting with delight. "A letter from Lilly!"

Oscar, forgetting his complaints, said happily, "Let's hear what she's got to say."

Mattie held the pink envelope up to the window, tore off an end, pulled out the letter, and read aloud, "Dear Ma. Do not read this letter to Pa...."

Oscar lifted his eyebrows and said, "Too late now. Read on."

Mattie's face fell, knowing he was right. She nodded and then began to read, aloud:

A warm breeze is coming through the kitchen window, fluttering the curtains you made for me. The crab trees on the boulevard are blooming, which makes me think of the orchard at home.

Not much rain here this spring, so the ground is nice and dry. I bet Pa is out plowing.

I love pretty much everything about nursing, except for the doctors, who strut around Cook County General like barnyard roosters, crowing orders. I wish you and Pa would visit. I'd get your advice on my sorry-looking houseplants, and I'd take Pa to Michigan Avenue, where he'd get a look at our city in the sky. A ninety-floor skyscraper, nicknamed "Big John," just opened.

Richard surprised me last week. He gave me an engagement ring, the same ring his father had given his mother, a single diamond set on a gold band worn thin.

We plan to be married on June 20, in Kiel – at Richard's church. I will ask Reverend Schreiber to assist Father Dorn with the ceremony. I hope you will want to sew my dress.

Break the news to Pa when he is in a good mood, and let me know how he takes it. I hope he will want to give me away.

Your happy daughter,
Lilly

Mattie refolded the letter, slipped it into the torn envelope, and looked at her husband, who stared out the window, beyond the field to the cattail swamp along the river. She slid the envelope to the center of the oilcloth-covered table, which made Oscar glance at it.

"Pretty soon she'll be writing us in Latin," he said.

"Oscar, Richard is a fine young man."

"A fine young *Catholic* man."

"We'll just have to accept that."

"Maybe *you* can." Oscar stood, walked out of the kitchen, and pulled on his work boots by the back door.

"Where are you going?" Mattie asked.

"Back to work."

"Supper is nearly ready."

"Never mind supper." He bent, laced up his boots, and let the screen door slam behind him.

Mattie sighed and said to herself, "Heaven help us." It was not like Oscar to skip a meal.

Oscar, still in shock, walked across the field, his heels sinking into the soft soil, the moist earth clinging to his soles like dark frosting on one of Mattie's cakes. He climbed onto the hot metal seat of his tractor and turned the ignition key. Nothing happened. Oscar did what Lutheran men do when surprised by their horses, tractors, or daughters – he swore. Every bad word Oscar knew came out of his mouth, a mix of German and English, one long sentence so filthy that you would not have wanted to be downwind from it.

He tried the ignition again, and the engine sparked and caught, obliterating the country quiet. Black exhaust raised the muffler cap and stunk up the air. Oscar lowered the plow and took his foot off the clutch. The tractor lurched ahead, as did his mind: How could she marry outside the faith? It's just not right. She's asking for trouble! he thought, tightening his grip on the tractor's black steering wheel.

Oscar, a purebred Protestant, traced his Lutheran heritage back to sixteenth-century Germany. All his relatives were Lutherans who married Lutherans, as he had: Mattie was the daughter of a Lutheran pastor. At family gatherings, Oscar's aunts and sisters recited passages from Luther's Long Catechism to their children, and when the children were off playing, Oscar's brothers and uncles told hard-edged stories and jokes about Catholic clerics.

The plow blades jumped. Oscar twisted around in his tractor seat and watched a forty-pound boulder come up from its ten-thousand-year-old resting place. He stopped the tractor, got off, and picked up the rock. Walking to the nearest stone fence, he set the rock in its new resting place.

As a boy, Oscar used to follow his father's fresh furrow, picking up rocks unearthed by the single plow blade, rolling the rocks to the edge of the field and laying them into the stone fence. In those days, every farmer laid and tended stone fences, but after the War, most of Oscar's neighbors had, in his words, "gone crazy for barbed wire," leaving their stone fences untended. Over the years, the frost and thaw had brought them down. But Oscar kept tending his stone fences, and everyone who drove by his farm noticed the waist-high ribbons of rock, the granite skeleton of his farm, each stone fitted into place like a brick.

That evening, Oscar and Mattie finished dinner and sat on the front-porch swing for the first time that season, their way to end a warm day. With the ball of his stockinged foot, Oscar gave the swing a lazy push every so often as the couple watched the dark come on. The sheep and chickens grew quiet. A light breeze carried the fragrance of apple blossoms and freshly turned earth.

Out on the highway, a red Dodge Charger passed the farm, its windows down, electric guitar riffs from the car's radio interrupting the evening quiet. Irritated, Oscar asked, "Who is that?"

"The Heinen boy."

"The one you tried to set up with Lilly?"

"Yaah."

The Charger turned the corner and roared south, toward Elkhart Lake. Oscar asked, "What's the matter with young people today? They play their music loud enough to wake the dead. They shoot holes in my *No Trespassing* sign down by the river ... and ..." His voice trailed off.

Mattie spoke his words: "And Lutheran girls fall in love with Catholic boys."

After a long silence, Oscar asked his wife, "You remember old lady Dunkelblau?"

"What on earth made you think of her?"

"When I was boy, I was sitting on the church steps one afternoon when along comes old lady Dunkelblau, her head down, watching where she put each foot. She stopped, looked at the church, frowned, spit, and made the sign of the cross. 'Why did you do that?' I asked. She said, 'To drive out them evil spirits.' I decided right then and there that *she* was an evil spirit and if she ever did that again, I'd drive her out.

"Few days later, she did the same thing, so I said, 'Frau Dunkelblau – you want to hear a little German rhyme I made up for you?'

"'*Gewiss*,' she said, nodding.

"So I said, in a voice as sweet as an angel:

Katholische Affen,
Im Butter gebraten,
Mit Mehl geschmirt,
Zum Teufel dafuhrt.

Mattie said, "Honestly!" and repeated the poem in English:

Catholic monkeys,
in butter fried,
and rolled in flour,
to the devil are sent.

Oscar asked, "Clever, yaah?"

"No," Mattie said. "Mean. What did Dunkelblau do?"

"Walked off. Next day she came back, set a plastic statue of Mary the Virgin on the church step, wagged her crooked finger at me, and said something in Latin, which spooked me so bad I stomped the statue to smitherines and ran away."

"*Rahaaaeoowww!* " A tomcat howled from the dark woods between the front porch and the highway into town.

Another tomcat answered with a low, fierce moan, "*Oawww-weoooww.*"

Mattie said, "Lutheran meets Catholic in the woods."

A moment later, the cats closed and fought, rolling in the underbrush, howling, screaming.

When the catfight ended, Mattie said, "I'm going to make Lilly her wedding dress. Am I going to have to give her away, too?"

Oscar pushed harder against the floor with his foot, and the swing began creaking. He said nothing, but in his mind, his quiet, deep love for his daughter collided with his disapproval of her intentions: How can I give her away? How can I not? People should marry their own kind!

"Well?" Mattie asked.

"Remember when you tried to set Lilly up with the Heinen boy, and I said, 'Don't do it, Mattie – stay out of her business?'"

"Yaah," Mattie said.

"I should have kept my mouth shut. Maybe she'd be marrying him now and we'd be planning a Lutheran wedding."

"With electric guitars playing, 'Here Comes the Bride,'" Mattie said.

Oscar woke up at midnight, cold. He turned onto his back and pulled the blanket up to his neck. An hour later, he woke up, hot. He threw off the blanket, turned onto his side, creased and doubled his pillow, and waited for sleep, which did not come. He had long awaited the day of escorting his daughter down the aisle, but he had always imagined that it would be the aisle at Trinity Lutheran, not the aisle at St. Peter and Paul. I don't even know what that aisle looks like, he thought.

At breakfast the next morning, Mattie studied her husband's trembling hands and bloodshot eyes. "You look awful," she said.

"Didn't sleep good."

"You take it easy today, Oscar."

After his barnyard chores, Oscar visited the wooden, weather-beaten outhouse he had built at the edge of the plowed field, his home away from home. He preferred the outdoor toilet to the indoor one, partly because he was a private man, and partly because when he used the indoor toilet, he felt rushed, even if no one else was in the house. When he sat in the outhouse, he felt relaxed, at ease, which helped his body do what it had to do and helped his mind wander freely, at least until it bumped into one of the stone fences which crisscrossed his brain.

He left the outhouse. Backing his tractor out of the barn, he drove it onto the field, stopping where he had quit the day before, and lowered his plow. As soon as Oscar's tractor lurched forward, its plow blades hooked a boulder so large that the tractor balked and the engine quit. Oscar swore, jumped down, grabbed his shovel, and began digging around the boulder, which showed only a white rounded top, like the bald crown of a giant buried skull.

The vigorous shovel work made Oscar a little light-headed, so he straightened up and closed his eyes, expecting to see a soothing dark. Instead, he saw – in his mind's eye – a bluebird flying above his plowed field, alighting on top of his outhouse and becoming a woman dressed in a hooded, blue robe pulled around her face, with eyes the color of the freshly turned soil. She stood on the outhouse as if it was her pedestal.

Oscar opened his eyes, shook his head hard enough to clap the inside of his cheeks against his molars, and looked at the outhouse – no bluebird, no woman. Am I losing my mind? he wondered. He closed his eyes and saw her again, her robe rippling in the breeze, her dark, kind face looking at him.

He opened his eyes and threw himself into the work at hand, not with the steady, measured pace which characterized his work – and his entire life – but with abandon and fury, as if unearthing that boulder would set his world in order. Oscar was a practical man, his life shaped by work and duty, not dreams or visions, so he did not know what to make of what he had just seen with his eyes shut. He plunged his shovel into the soil, grunted, lifted, cursed, and flung each shovelful of dirt over his head, the soil scattering in the air and landing behind him, again and again.

Mattie watched him from the kitchen window, worried about how he was acting. She phoned the church and said, "May I speak with Reverend Schreiber, please?"

Reverend Schreiber got on the phone and said, "I've been expecting your call, Mattie," he said. Two days earlier, he had also received a letter from Lilly.

"Come right away," she said. "Oscar didn't take the news well."

The boulder was bigger than Oscar had expected. It took him ten minutes to dig around and under it, and by the time he had it fully exposed, his chest heaved, sweat ran into his eyes, and Mattie and Reverend Schreiber stood in the driveway, watching him work.

Oscar threw the shovel aside, wiped his forehead with his sleeve, kneeled, grunted, and began to roll the hundred-pound rock out of the hole and across the field. Staying on his knees, he rolled the boulder to the nearest stone fence.

"Look at him, Reverend," Mattie said, alarmed.

Oscar rearranged a number of rocks on the stone fence, making a space for the boulder. He bent down, got his arms around the boulder, grunted, and jerked it to his waist. Turning, he dropped it into the space he had created, pleased by the sound of the heavy boulder gouging the smaller rocks.

The noon whistle of the factory west of town wailed. Oscar looked up, surprised to see Reverend Schreiber's navy Plymouth in the driveway – and alongside it, Schreiber and Mattie, both waving him in for lunch. He glanced at the outhouse one more time before heading for the farmhouse.

At lunch, Reverend Schreiber asked, "What were you doing with that boulder, Oscar?"

"Mending my fence."

"Ah! When I was a school boy, I memorized Robert Frost's 'Mending Wall,' a poem he wrote about stone fences like yours." Schreiber closed his eyes and began to recite the poem, happy that the words came back to him:

> *Something there is that doesn't love a wall,*
> *That sends the frozen-ground-swell under it*
> *And spills the upper boulders in the sun,*
> *And makes gaps even two can pass abreast.*

Schreiber's mouth hung open, ready to recite the next stanza, but the words did not come to him. He paused, shook his head, and said, "That's all that comes back."

That's plenty, Oscar thought.

"My husband writes poetry, too." Mattie said, smiling. "Why don't you recite your poem to Reverend Schreiber?"

Oscar frowned at her, turned to his pastor, and said, "I wrote one poem in my entire life and that was to spite an old lady and her religion."

Schreiber lifted his coffee cup to his lips, sipped, and clinked his cup back onto its saucer. "I got a letter from Lilly this week," he said.

Oscar looked at him, knowing now why he had come.

"Lilly asked me to assist Father Dorn with her wedding."

"You ever done such a thing?" Oscar asked him.

"I've gone fishing with Father Dorn, but I've never done a wedding with him."

"You going to do it?"

"Yes."

Oscar nodded, looked out the window and studied the outhouse, its door swinging open and shut in the stiffening May breeze.

After lunch, Oscar walked Reverend Schreiber to his car, and the men made small talk about the weather. Just before Schreiber got in his car, Oscar cleared his throat and said, "We got to talk, Lutheran to Lutheran."

"I understand," Schreiber said, sure that Oscar was finally going to reveal his misgivings about his daughter's marriage.

Oscar looked at Schreiber's polished black shoes against the white pea gravel and said, "You're going to lose that shine."

"Where are we going?"

"Follow me," Oscar said, turning. He walked along the edge of his plowed field, stopping by the boulder he had hefted on top of his old stone fence. "See anything unusual out there, Reverend?"

Schreiber, a little confused, studied the scene and said, "River looks low."

"Never mind the river. Look at my outhouse."

"What about it?" Schreiber asked, chuckling.

"Close your eyes."

Schreiber glanced at Oscar, then closed his eyes.

"Now what do you see?"

"The inside of my eyelids."

"Oh," Oscar said.

Schreiber opened his eyes and looked at Oscar, puzzled.

"Earlier today," Oscar said, "I stood here, closed my eyes, and saw a woman with a blue robe standing on top of my outhouse."

Schreiber tilted his head, and asked, "You saw this with your eyes closed?"

"Yaah."

"Did you recognize this woman?" Schreiber asked.

"Yaah. Mary."

Thinking first of Oscar's neighbor, Schreiber asked, "Mary Hoppel?"

"MarythemotherofJesusforGod'ssake!"

Schreiber took a step back from Oscar, glancing again at the outhouse before he spoke:

"Oscar, I don't see things with my eyes closed. I baptize babies. Visit the sick. Read the Bible – I do it all with my eyes wide open. I even pray with my eyes open."

Oscar sat on the boulder.

Schreiber laid his hand on Oscar's shoulder and said, "You might have had a vision, Oscar. Then again ... you might have had a nervous breakdown."

Oscar put his face in his hands.

Schreiber offered a referral: "Go see Father Dorn. Tell him I sent you."

After Reverend Schreiber had gone, Oscar and Mattie went straight upstairs for their daily *mittagpause* – naptime. Oscar did not want to close his eyes, but as his body relaxed, his eyelids closed. Half an hour later, Mattie sat up on the bed, stretched, and looked at her husband, his hands folded across his chest, his fingers twitching, his flat stomach rising and falling, sound asleep.

Oscar slept all afternoon, until the wind blew his bedroom door shut: *Bang!* He opened his eyes, sat up in bed, threw his feet to the floor, and looked out the bedroom window. Apple blossoms from the orchard blew through the air like huge snowflakes. Oscar glanced at the wind-up clock by his bedside. He shook his head, stood, and hurried down the hall in his stockinged feet, smelling fried sausage and sauerkraut.

"That was some nap!" Mattie said, glancing at the kitchen clock as Oscar came into the kitchen. "You got up just in time for dinner."

Oscar sat in his chair. "That was no nap," he said. "That was hibernation."

Mattie set out a plate of sausage and sauerkraut, a loaf of thick-crusted bread, and a bowl of pink applesauce on the table. As soon as she sat, the couple bowed their heads and folded their hands over their empty plates. Surprising both himself and Mattie, Oscar reached across the table and laid his left hand over his wife's hands before he began grace, bowing his head but keeping his eyes open.

That evening, it was too windy to sit on the porch, so Oscar and Mattie sat in the front room. He read the comics without chuckling, then folded his hands in his lap and watched his wife knit. She was making something tiny, with snow-white yarn.

"What's that?" Oscar asked.

"Baby bootie."

"For who?"

"Our first grandchild," she said, without looking up.

"Better make a couple dozen," Oscar said. "Catholics have big families."

At nine o'clock, Mattie held up the pair of white booties and said, "Time for bed."

"You go," Oscar said. "I slept all afternoon. I'll be up later, after the news."

Oscar never turned on the television, never watched the news. Instead, he switched off all the lights in the house and walked onto the dark porch. A gust of wind came around the porch corner and tossed Oscar's hair into his eyes. I'll go for a walk, he thought, maybe that'll do me good. He stepped off the porch and into the night and wind without any destination in mind. He walked down the driveway, under the overhanging basswood and maple, the wind clacking the branches against each other like wooden swords.

At the end of the driveway, he lifted a small, round rock, the size of a hen's egg, from his stone fence and looked both ways down the empty asphalt highway. Putting his back to the wind, he walked toward town, turning the smooth stone over and over with his thick, short fingers.

Twenty minutes later, Oscar sat on Trinity's front steps – where he had first met Frau Dunkelblau. Just across Main Street, the twin, tall steeples of St. Peter and Paul stood against the black sky, illuminated by white spotlights. Warm, yellow light poured out of the rectory's front-room window onto the sidewalk.

Oscar looked up and down Main Street. Nothing moved, except for last year's torn and brittle leaves blowing and scraping along the street. Down by the railroad tracks, a green neon light, shaped like a martini glass, reflected off the hoods of several cars parked beneath it.

A man in his robe and slippers opened the rectory door, came out, closed the door behind him, and stood on the front steps. Oscar watched him. The man dipped his head and lit a cigarette, the tiny yellow flame revealing his face. The cigarette glowed red each time the man raised it to his lips.

Oscar stood and walked across Main Street.

"Who goes there?" asked Father Dorn.

"Oscar Stickler."

"Oscar! You're the only farmer in these parts still on your feet."

"Couldn't sleep."

"The wind, no doubt."

"No."

Father Dorn took a drag on his cigarette and asked, "Were you waiting for me?"

Oscar did not reply.

Father Dorn crushed his cigarette on the rectory's brick wall, flicked it onto the street, and walked down the steps. "Is this about your daughter's marriage?"

"Today, I was out plowing. I shut my eyes and a woman came to me."

"A woman?"

"In a blue robe."

Astonished, Father Dorn said, "The Blessed Mother came to you!"

"No. She came to my outhouse!"

Dorn laughed and said, "Her ways are a mystery."

"Why did I see her?"

Father Dorn quieted and looked at Oscar. "Your suffering drew her near you."

Oscar stood for a long time without speaking, taking in the exchange with the priest.

Oscar nodded toward Father Dorn's church and asked, "Is it open?"

"We never lock it."

"Could I get a look inside?"

"Certainly." Father Dorn led Oscar up the church steps and pulled open a tall, thick door. The sweet, pungent odor of burned incense poured out of the dark building, as if it had been waiting just inside the door for a chance to escape into the night sky, and the wind blew through the open doorway, as if it had been waiting to get inside the empty church.

Oscar stepped through the open door. The immense room held mostly darkness, but he could make out rows of pews ahead of him, divided by a wide aisle leading to a dozen flickering candles on an altar made of stone. Father Dorn propped open the door, joined Oscar, and said, "I'll turn on some lights." His words echoed around the great room as if in a cave.

"No," whispered Oscar. "Wait here." He walked forward, down the very aisle his daughter would walk at her wedding. His footsteps echoed above and around him. Oscar made it to the altar, reached in his pocket, laid the round, smooth stone from his fence upon the stone altar, turned, and walked back down the aisle. Both men walked through the door and stood again on the church steps.

The priest lit another cigarette, inhaled, exhaled, and said, "I wouldn't tell too many Catholics about what you saw, Oscar. You might start a worldwide pilgrimage to your outhouse."

Father Dorn chuckled, but Oscar did not. He closed his eyes and had a second vision even more troubling than his first – his farm as a Catholic Holy Shrine, with hundreds of cars parked in his field and a crowd of foreigners surrounding his outhouse and chanting, in Latin. Oscar shuddered, opened his eyes, and said, "Not another word, Father," offering his hand to the priest.

The men shook hands, and Oscar turned away and walked back down Main Street, toward home, unable to remember the last time he'd been in town at night. On the Sheboygan River bridge, Oscar paused and looked down at the river, thinking, Reverend Schreiber was right – low for this time of year.

As Oscar approached his farm, he saw yellow light pouring through the kitchen windows and onto the dark lawn. Mattie's up too, he thought. He walked into the kitchen, where his wife was sitting in her chair, dressed in her bedclothes, both hands holding a glass of cold milk. Walking to the phone, he tore off a sheet of note paper, picked up a ballpoint pen, and sat in his chair, his left knee again finding her right knee under the table.

"It bothers me too, Oscar," she said.

"I know."

"Are you going to write her?"

He nodded and put on his glasses.

She sipped her milk and watched him write the letter, but she could not see what he wrote, and she did not ask, figuring that if he wanted her to know, he'd read it to her. The wind rattled the windows, and the kitchen clock struck a steady beat towards morning.

When Oscar was done, he set down the pen and read, softly:

Dear Lilly,

Finished plowing today. Ground looks good. Lots of stones came up, so I got fence mending ahead.

A big wind blew this afternoon and carried the apple blossoms into the sky – I woke up from my nap and thought it was snowing!

Your Ma told me about your wedding. She's so happy she already knit a pair of baby booties, said she'll sew you any kind of wedding dress you want.

I don't go for you marrying outside our faith, but that ain't going to stop me from walking you down that aisle.

I even practiced once, just to see if I could do it.

Love,
Pa.

BUCK HAVEN

THE THREE MEN SAT HIP TO HIP in Ben's forest-green pickup, heading north, watching the eastern sky brighten. Each man wore a red-and-black plaid shirt, green wool trousers held up by blaze orange suspenders, and felt-lined leather boots. Ben, a retired hatcheryman from Elkhart Lake, glanced often at the world behind him in his big square rearview mirror, his hands at ten and two o'clock on the steering wheel. Fritz, a Lake to Lake Dairy retiree from Kiel, rode the hump, a block of cheddar warming in his shirt pocket. Spike, a retired shopkeeper from Sheboygan, rode shotgun, a steel thermos of coffee between his legs.

Fritz checked his pocketwatch and said, "Should be there by noon."

Each year, for the last thirty years, the men had met before dawn on the Friday before Thanksgiving and lived the next ten days as close to one another as most men dare. In the spring of 1956, they had bought twenty acres of swamp and woods "up north" in Oconto Country, along County W, each man paying a thousand dollars for joint title. During July of that year, they had pitched a tent on the highest spot of that twenty acres, swatted mosquitoes, and built their hunting cabin, assisted by Fritz's son, Dennis, a skinny, nervous boy just shy of thirteen. Each night, the men had stripped naked and examined one another for wood ticks. And each night, Dennis had kept his clothes on and turned his back, not ready to face his father and father's friends grooming each other like chimpanzees.

Early in their marriages, Ben, Fritz, and Spike had figured that a good God would bless hunters with sons upon sons. But Dennis was the only son born to the three men. The men had built the cabin as much for him as for themselves. But Dennis, in a turn of events which created further doubts about the goodness of God, had never again returned to the cabin after that first summer. His abiding absence troubled the men. They looked upon Dennis as their one and only chance to pass along the kind of manliness which hungered for big woods, fine rifles, and keen wits to match against the most magnificent animal in the north, the whitetail buck.

Each year, on the drive north, Fritz spoke about his son, in a tone which blended defeat and apology: "Dennis has got play practice at school, says he can't miss it." Or, "Dennis says shooting a big buck isn't what his new college friends talk about."

One year it was, "Gol damn Dennis has got a girlfriend this year, can't stand to have her out of his sight. He better watch himself with her. I've seen the way she looks at him."

The next year, "She got to him. Dennis is going to marry that girl, Margie, and move to the Twin Cities with her. Oh – and get this – she used to hunt deer with her dad and brothers in Illinois, if that don't beat all."

Last year, Ben had pretty well closed the long-standing conversation about Dennis by saying, "I figure there's a gene for deer hunting that gets passed on, father to son, but it must be one of them recessive genes – like blue eyes. Face it – we can't make Dennis' eyes turn blue and we can't make him want to hunt."

Spike had three daughters and Fritz had one daughter, but it had never occurred to either of them to invite their daughters to the cabin. Ben and his wife had no living children. They had lost their only child, a baby born with a bad heart, a girl, three days after her birth. As far as the men knew, no girl, no woman, had ever set foot on their land.

Just south of Green Bay, the men stopped for breakfast at the Finer Diner, a roadside coffee shop. The truckers sat at stools along the counter, their backs to the highway. The farmers sat in window booths, looking out across the fields. The deer hunters sat at square tables between the truckers and farmers – forty patrons, a full restaurant, all men, laughing, stirring sugar and cream into black coffee, mopping up egg yolks with toast crust.

When Ben, Fritz, and Spike entered the diner, Mr. Fine, owner and cook, turned from his griddle, smiled at them, and nodded. In honor of the deer hunters, Mr. Fine had spray painted his hat with blaze orange paint. "Sit anywhere, fellas!" he shouted, happily. "One of my girls will be right with you."

The men sat at a red formica table and reviewed the menu. A teen-age girl with straight blonde hair, short skirt, nylons, and comfortable shoes turned over their coffee mugs. She poured coffee, set the pot on the table, and took out her order pad and pencil. Fritz said, "Gol damn bacon sure smells good – bacon, two eggs looking at me, white toast."

Ben said, "Same for me."

Spike said, "Short stack and sausage." The waitress took the coffee pot, spun on her soft heels, and headed to another table.

After the men had finished breakfast, Fritz said, "She's the same waitress we had last year. But she wasn't quite as … developed."

"She's developed alright, but she hasn't picked up any speed," Ben said, eager to get the check and hit the road. "No big tip for her," he added.

Spike said, "Ben, you never met a tip you couldn't shrink."

"She's the last woman we'll see for ten days," Fritz said. "Let's treat her right and each give her a George Washington!" Each man stuck a dollar, face up, under his plate.

North of Green Bay, the land began to change: red barns, white farmhouses, wood lots, and corn-stubble fields gave way to pine, spruce, and hemlock forest which covered the land like a carpet all the way to Hudson Bay, unbroken except for lakes, roads, small towns, potato farms, and hunting camps. The change in the land created a restlessness in the men's bodies. Ben rolled down his window, rolled it up, rolled it down, turned off the heater, turned it on. Spike laced up his boots, ready to hit the ground. Fritz quit talking and watched the woods for deer.

At eleven o'clock, Ben drove into the northwoods town of Crivitz and turned left onto County W, a two-lane asphalt road laid through the forest. "My Ford knows the way from here," he said. Ten minutes later, the three men, eyes wide, turned onto a little forest lane and bounced across fallen tree branches, old tire ruts, and a tiny, rocky creek.

Their cabin wasn't much to look at from the outside, just rolls of green shingle tarpaper nailed over sheets of plywood. Above the door hung a wooden sign with hand-carved, irregular letters:

BUCK HAVEN. Ben drove his pickup alongside the cabin and parked. The men got out, stretched, and looked around, pulling the spruce-spiced air deep into their lungs.

Spike headed down a leaf-littered footpath to the outhouse. Fritz got an armful of hemlock logs and spruce kindling from last year's woodpile. Ben walked to the front door, pulled out a little silver key, unlocked the padlock, pushed the door open, and stepped inside the dark cabin.

Inside: one room, fifteen by twenty feet, three small windows, a cast-iron wood stove. Against one wall: three double bunks. Against another wall: a pine plank counter crisscrossed by ten thousand knife marks, and a white porcelain sink with a handpump. An uneven pine plank table sat in the middle of the cabin, surrounded by six wobbly stools. Ben sniffed the stale air, heavy with the odors of dry rot, moss, and mice.

Ben hung his coat on the tip of a spread of antlers mounted alongside the door, a perfect ten-point rack from his 1966 buck. Fritz set his armful of wood by the stove, crumpled up a newspaper from November 20th of the year before, and laid a fire in the stove. Spike took out the last of his cheddar cheese, cut six little cubes, and set a half a dozen mouse traps: one in each cabin corner, one under the sink, and one behind the wood stove. Using an old broom, Ben pulled down corner cobwebs and swept the floor.

Darkness came early in late November. At four o'clock, Ben lit the kerosene lantern, Fritz added a small log to the stove, and Spike began to shave the skins and warts off long, crisp carrots. All at once, each man held still and listened to a vehicle on County W slow, stop, back up, and turn down their lane. Spike asked, "Anyone expecting visitors?" The men shook their heads. Ben picked up the lantern and Fritz, who had just last week watched *Deliverance*, a movie about backwoods violence, lifted his unloaded 30-30 off the wall rack.

The three men stepped outside and watched a station wagon bounce up the lane toward them. When the car made the last turn before the cabin, its headlight beams illuminated the men like deer in a poacher's spotlight. The station wagon stopped. The driver turned off the engine.

The men waited, squinting into the headlights, expecting to see or hear a car door open, but no door opened. Fritz whispered, "I don't like this." He reached in his pocket for a cartridge and without looking down, pushed it into the chamber of his rifle. Still no one got out of the car, which spooked Fritz so bad that he shouted, "Come out with your hands up, whoever you are!"

The driver's side window rolled down and a man's voice shouted, "Pa!"

Fritz answered. "Gol damn, Dennis! What are you doing here?" Fritz wondered if middle-age had activated the latent hunting gene in his son.

The car's passenger window rolled down and a woman's voice shouted, "Don't shoot!"

Ben and Spike looked at Fritz, who shouted, "Margie? ... Tell Dennis to shut off them damn headlights unless he intends to poach us!"

Dennis chuckled, turned off the lights, and hollered, "We thought we'd surprise you."

The three men answered in unison, like a chorus in a Greek tragedy, "You did."

Dennis and Margie got out of the car and greeted the men,

who sized up Margie in the lantern light. She was a woman of thirty-five, fit, slender, wearing heavy boots and the longest brown hair that had ever been in that deer camp. Ben set down the lantern and shook Dennis' hand, happy to see him back at Buck Haven. A moment later, he extended his hand to Margie, who shook his hand with such unexpected vigor that it threw him off balance. Fritz asked Margie, "Where are the kids, then?"

"Staying with my folks."

"You two had supper?" Fritz asked, glancing at his son, removing the cartridge from his rifle and slipping it back into his pants pocket.

"We're so hungry we could eat a deer!" Dennis said, his eyes reflecting the lantern glow.

"My son – late for everything but supper!" Fritz turned, opened the cabin door, and added, "Everybody inside!"

Dennis and Margie entered the cabin first, pausing just inside the door, looking, sniffing. Dennis said to his wife, "I helped build this shack when I was a kid."

His father, coming in behind him, stuck his finger in his son's back as if it were a rifle barrel and said, "A shack is where you put your lawn mower, son. This is a cabin. This is Buck Haven."

Dennis walked across the pine plank floor to one of the bunks, pointed to a carving in the board just above the bunk, and read it aloud, "Dennis was here. 1956." He followed Spike to the sink, picked up one of the shaven carrots, bit off the tip, and munched. Margie walked to the stove and rubbed her hands in its heat.

Fritz turned to his son and asked, in a casual tone which disguised his hope, "You going to join us for the hunt, then?"

"Me?" he asked, pointing a carrot at his chest. "Sorry, Pa. I'll stay the night, but I got to get back to the Cities tomorrow."

"You came all the way from Minneapolis just to say hello, eat, and run off?" Fritz asked, puzzled.

Dennis glanced at his wife and said, "I came to say hello to you three old farts and bring Margie. She'd like to hunt with you guys."

The men looked at Dennis, trying to take in what was just said.

When Margie spoke, all of their heads turned to her. "I used to hunt with my dad and brothers."

Fritz, eager to talk her out of such an idea, said, "Let me get this straight. You want to stay in a one-room 'shack' with three old farts for ten days and ten nights?"

Laughing, she said, "Sounds like heaven to me!"

Fritz added, "Heaven with an outhouse, mice, and wood rats!"

She laughed again, not the reaction he expected. Fritz was stuck. He could not think of a way to say no to his daughter-in-law, and he could not think of a way to work a woman into life at Buck Haven.

Ben, the eldest, stepped in to manage the crisis. He looked at Spike and asked, "Old fart number one, what do you say?"

Spike drew on his work history for a reply: "When we hired the first woman at Lake to Lake, it was rougher on her than on us. If Margie wants to hunt with us, I say we give it a try."

Ben nodded, turned to Fritz, and asked, "Old fart number two?"

A hemlock log crackled and popped in the stove.

"These guys tell me I snore like a bear," Fritz said.

Margie replied, "Your son tells me I snore, too."

Fritz said, "Well, if you still want to join us ..."

"I do," she said.

"Watch out, guys!" Dennis added. "She said those two words to me once on the altar and she meant them!"

"What about you, Ben?" Margie asked.

Hiding his misgivings, he said, "Take the top bunk on the right, just above my bunk."

Fritz looked at Margie and said, "You get a set of chores, just like the rest of us."

"Fair enough," she said. "I'll get my stuff."

"I'll help," said Dennis, following his wife out of the cabin.

Dennis opened the back of the station wagon and took out his wife's purple sleeping bag, pink pillow, and mauve suitcase. Margie took out her gun case, along with her matching red wool coat and pants. Back in the cabin, they piled her gear on her bunk, and she took a flashlight out of the suitcase. "Which direction to the Ladies Room?" she asked, smiling.

The three men pointed south. Ben said, "I'll walk you there, it's hard to find in the dark." He put on his coat, handed her an unopened roll of toilet paper, opened the door, and led Margie into the woods.

Margie entered the outhouse and shut the door. Ben didn't feel right about standing right outside the door, but he didn't feel right about leaving her alone in the woods either. So he turned his back to the outhouse, walked off a dozen steps, stopped, and waited. Ahead of him, the lantern light poured through the cabin window and a ribbon of white smoke rose from the chimney.

Behind him, he heard more than he wanted to hear. Margie put down the wooden seat, slid down her pants, sat, and hollered, "Ooooooooooooo!" as her rear touched the cold wood. A moment later, her stream of pee pelted the soft mush at the bottom of the pit. It seemed to Ben that she peed for forty days and forty nights, and he wondered to himself, what's she got inside her, a fifty-five gallon drum? When she hit empty, he heard her tear open the roll of toilet paper.

Back in the cabin, Spike set a skillet on the stove, Ben set the table, and Margie unrolled her sleeping bag. Dennis and Fritz sat in wooden rockers, and son said to father, "I know you wish I'd stay, Pa, but it's not in me to hunt."

Disappointed, Fritz held his tongue.

Forty minutes later, Spike put a pot of stew, a loaf of unsliced bread, and a pint jar of raspberry jam on the table. "Dinner's getting cold," he announced. The four men and Margie each found a stool around the table and Spike passed a yellowed, torn piece of cardboard to Ben.

Ben took the cardboard, put on his reading glasses, and said, "Dennis – I wrote this poem years ago. We read it each year, a prayer of sorts." He looked at Margie and added, "No woman's ever heard it."

"First time for everything," Margie said.

Ben cleared his throat and read, aloud:

> *Here at Buck Haven,*
> *Whenever we eat,*
> *We ain't combed or clean-shaved,*
> *but we're thankful for meat.*
>
> *We're in the northwoods,*
> *where God meant us to be,*

No wives, phones, or "shoulds,"
No right place to pee.

So we pray for the buck,
Big rack, fine and fleet,
And we ask for good luck
In this week, short but sweet.

And he concluded, "Now, good God, let's eat!"

Dennis laughed and said, "I never figured this shack ... excuse me – this cabin ... would inspire poetry!"

Ben, embarrassed, set down the poem, grabbed the pot of stew, held it out for Margie, and said, "Ladies first."

It was an awkward moment, and Margie knew that she had to say something. "It's not ladies first for anything this week," she said. "I'm just a deer hunter, like all you, okay?"

After dinner, Ben put a pot of water on the stove for dishes, and Fritz revised the chore list, adding Margie to the daily round of woodsplitting, sweeping, cooking, and dishwashing. He tacked it on the wall, and said, "First one up lights a fire. Last one standing feeds the fire and shuts off the lantern. Margie, you got dishes tonight."

Dennis looked at his wife and said, "You wash. I'll dry."

At eight o'clock, Ben, Fritz, and Spike got out their rifles. Ben oiled the walnut stock of his Remington .308. Spike greased the bolt of his old Springfield 30-'06. Fritz checked the lever action on his Winchester 30-30. Each man, if asked, could explain why he used that rifle and not another, with details about caliber, action, barrel, magazine, sights, accuracy, cartridges, and memories.

Margie walked to her bunk, unzipped her gun case, and pulled out a long-barreled, twelve-gauge shotgun, which surprised the men. Spike glanced at Ben and Fritz and asked her, "You going to hunt ducks or deer?"

"My dad died last year," she replied. "This was his gun, which he used for ducks and deer. My brothers wanted me to have it. So now, it's mine. I think of Dad whenever I hold it...." Like the men, she had her reasons for using that gun and not another. Margie added, "I want to thank you guys for letting me hunt with you this year," glancing at each man.

Ben found himself taking an unexpected interest in Margie. He watched how she held her dad's shotgun, and how she oiled the stock. He listened to her voice lower when she spoke to her husband and rise when she spoke to anyone else. Later, he watched her brush her hair, easing her stroke whenever she hit a tangle. At first, he worried that his interest might be carnal, but he shook that worry out of his mind by reminding himself, you're old enough to be her father!

"Ever shot a deer?" Ben asked her.

"I shot *at* a deer once," Margie answered.

"We best tell you how we hunt these big woods," Ben said.

She nodded, and Ben and the others began telling her about Buck Haven routine: rise at five, dress, eat, take a stand where two deer-trails cross, lean against a tree, move one's eyes and toes freely, move anything else only in order to keep it from freezing solid. Back to the cabin by noon. Eat. Nap. Drive the cedar swamps in early afternoon. Back to the stand until closing. Dinner. Stories. Bed.

Margie asked, "Will one of you show me where to take a stand?"

Ben said, "I'll put you on a good stand near me."

Fritz looked at Ben, surprised by his prompt invitation and relieved that he didn't have to assume solo responsibility for his daughter-in-law.

By nine o'clock, the old farts were ready for bed, but they stalled, not sure how to undress with a woman in the cabin. Ben thought, maybe I should hang a blanket for a dressing curtain, but Margie took the lead, stretched, and said, "Good night."

She walked to her husband, kissed his cheek, stripped to her body-tight thermal underwear, and in bare feet climbed the ladder to her bunk. The men did the same, and Ben, the last one standing, added two logs to the fire, turned out the lantern, stripped to his baggy longjohns, and got in his bunk, underneath Margie.

The bark from the fresh logs caught fire, crackling and sizzling. A mouse trap snapped shut behind the stove. A pack of coyotes yipped on the ridge behind the cabin, a wild, lonely sound, followed by another wild, lonely sound: Margie's first snore.

That night, Ben dreamt of his lost daughter for the first time in twenty years, not like he had known her, as a desperately ill infant, but like he had never known her, as a young woman.

Ben was the first to get up. He stirred the glowing coals in the stove with a poker and added wood, thinking of his dream. Lighting a lantern, he ran the cabin trapline, opened the door, and tossed three stiff mouse carcasses onto the frozen leaves. Margie was up next, still able to see her breath, shivering. She joined Ben by the stove in her bare feet and underwear, rubbed her palms against one another, and watched him crack eggs into a bowl.

"You hear them brush wolves on the ridge last night?" Ben

asked, without looking up.

"Didn't hear a thing," she said, adding, "Did I snore?"

Ben pulled apart the eggshell he had just cracked in half, let the egg plop into the bowl, and said, "A little."

The others stirred, yawned, and stretched. Fritz got up and touched his son's bare shoulder. Dennis opened his eyes, blinked, laid his hand across his father's hand and said, "Pa. I'm not getting up till it gets light. Good luck!"

By six o'clock, Ben, Fritz, Spike, and Margie were standing behind the cabin in the dark, directly beneath the pole used to hang and cure their deer. No one spoke.

Spike adjusted his suspenders until the stretch was just right. Fritz buttoned up his parka and counted the loose cartridges in his cargo pocket. Ben zipped up his blaze orange coveralls, a tropical color out of place on a man who usually wore beige or gray, but a color which kept other hunters from mistaking him for a deer. Margie looked up: clear, black sky, with galaxies of glittering stars, as if God had taken a bucket of light, froze it solid, shattered it into a million tiny pieces, and heaved the sparkling pieces across the heavens.

For Margie's benefit, Fritz gave parting instructions: "Fire three shots in the air if you need help or get lost. Good luck. Stay safe." He shined his light at the empty deer pole above them and added, "Let's see if we can hang a buck on this by nightfall."

He and the others walked off into the dark forest, knowing that Dennis would soon awaken, leave for the Twin Cities, and return the following weekend to pick up his wife. Fritz had left a note on the table for his son, which read, "I'm real happy you came back to visit us at Buck Haven. Drive safe. We'll take good care of Margie."

Ben walked through the woods and along the ridge where the coyotes had run, with Margie two steps behind him. He stopped at the highest spot on that ridge, kicked away a small circle of dry leaves, and whispered, "Stand here. Keep your mouth shut and eyes open. I'll be on the next ridge. When it gets light, we'll be able to see each other." He walked down the ridge, up the next ridge, and made his stand.

The stars faded, the sky brightened, and a lone raven flew overhead, as silent and black as the sky had been just an hour earlier. Far off, a rifle's sharp report echoed between ridges, the first shot of the season. Ben loaded his rifle.

As he pushed the fifth and final cartridge into his magazine, his whole body jumped at the deep blast of Margie's shotgun. The boom rolled across the woods, scattering the roosting songbirds in the tree above Ben. JesusGodinheaven! he wondered. What's she shooting at, ducks?

"Ben! Come quick!" Margie shouted, as if in trouble.

He hurried to her, breathing hard by the time he saw her standing where he had left her.

"Thank God you're all right!" he shouted. "I thought you shot yourself!"

She pointed at the body of a deer lying motionless on the ground near her.

"Well, I'll be ..."

The animal exhaled sharply, rattling its black nostrils, startling Ben and Margie. Ben pointed his rifle at the buck, and watched it through his rifle sights for a minute or two before saying, "That was his last breath."

He stepped forward, dropped to his knees, stroked the deer's coarse neck-hair, and studied the animal. "A forkhorn, Margie. A fine, fat forkhorn!" He glanced down at his watch. "My God! The season's been open five minutes and you got your buck!" Ben pointed to the entry wound of the slug, just behind the buck's front shoulder. "Heart shot."

She turned away, suddenly, as if repulsed by something.

"What's wrong?" he asked.

"I never killed a big, beautiful animal before."

"You said it yourself, Margie. First time for everything."

"Shut up!" she said, "and pour me a cup of coffee."

Ben turned and pulled his thermos from his game pocket, unscrewed the thermos top, and filled it with black, steaming coffee, which he held out to her.

"Just a minute," she said, reaching into her back pocket and pulling out a slender, aluminum flask. Seeing Ben's astonished look, she added, "This is the last of Dad's Irish whiskey. I figured I might need it if I actually shot a deer." She poured a shot into the coffee, sat down on the frozen, dry leaves, and raised her cup in the air, "To you, Dad."

Ben nodded and sat next to her.

After her first sip, she passed him the cup. He sniffed, took a sip, swallowed, and opened his eyes wide, the smell of burnt gunpowder, warm blood, coffee, whiskey, and musk mixing in the air around them.

"I loved my dad, Ben, but he wasn't easy to love. He drank, and when he drank, he got ugly."

Ben looked at Margie, taking in her comment. Far off, another rifle shot. Above them, a red pine squirrel with a white belly jumped from branch to branch, making its way across the naked forest canopy. A nuthatch flew to a beech tree near them, clung to the tree's trunk with its white rump pointed toward the sky, and looked down on them with tiny black eyes: "*Ank. Ank.*"

"I don't know the first thing about dressing out a deer, Ben."

"You want me to do it?" he asked.

"No.... But show me how."

"Take off your coat. Roll up your sleeves," Ben said. He turned the heavy, limp carcass of the buck onto its back and sat on it, bracing it between his legs, tying off the testicles and penis with a hunk of twine so that they wouldn't drain. Margie took out her pocket knife, but Ben said, "Put that away. Use mine. It handles better on a big animal."

At his instruction, she slid the knife into the buck's anus, cut a slit, pressed her fingers between hide and gut, and slit the animal from anus to brisket. Pink, green, and gray organs, steaming with body heat, bulged into the slit behind her fingers.

By the time she was done, hot, sticky blood coated her arms up to her elbows, and she stunk of musk. Ben took a rag out of his cargo pocket, wiped off her arms, and said, "Good work."

"Reminds me of giving birth," she said. "Blood and goop."

He surprised her with his next comment. "You're lucky you have children, Margie."

"Yes, I know. Do you have children?" she asked.

Ben usually said, "No," when asked this question, but he said, "I have a daughter."

"Oh! She must be about my age," Margie said.

"She would be.... We lost her not long after she was born."

"Oh – I'm so sorry."

The white-breasted nuthatch on the tree near them spoke again, "*Ank. Ank. Ank.*"

"What is your daughter's name, Ben?"

Ben could not answer. He looked into the ravine and shook his head.

"Say her name."

He looked at Margie, his voice breaking as he said, "Annie."

She picked up the cup of cold coffee laced with whiskey and raised it above her head, a toast to his daughter.

"I miss her terrible," Ben said. "I wonder what she would have been like." He looked at Margie and added, "Maybe she'd have been a young, beautiful woman – like you."

Margie smiled and added, "A deer hunter?"

"Maybe," Ben said, "if she had the right gene."

"*Ank. Ank.*"

Ben looked up at the nuthatch, which clung upside down to the tree trunk and watched him with tiny black eyes. Ben smiled, stood, and picked up his rifle. The bird flew to another tree. Ben fired three times into the air, a message to Spike and Fritz, though the shots reminded Margie of a military salute to a fallen soldier.

"Spike and Fritz will be here soon," he said.

"I got to pee like you wouldn't believe," Margie said.

"Oh, I believe it," Ben said. "I've heard what you can do," and he turned his back so that she could have the woods to herself.

GOOD MORNING, MR. AND MRS. AMERICA
AND ALL THE SHIPS AT SEA

Edna stood at her mother's kitchen counter, buttering a thick, soft slice of potato bread for her father's lunch, thinking about what to do with her life now that her high-school diploma was taped to her bedroom mirror and her classroom days were behind her.

In the front room, her parents stood next to the floor radio, their quiet voices mingling with the radio announcer's morning banter. Just after the seven o'clock tone, her father turned up the radio volume, and the family listened for the voice known to all Americans by its staccato delivery, patriotic commentary, and distinctive sign-on, the voice of a Hollywood gossip columnist turned news reporter:

"Good morning, Mr. and Mrs. America and all the ships at sea! This is Walter Winchell reporting from New York. Today is Tuesday, June 24th, 1941. Flash! – Hitler betrays his nonaggression pact with Stalin and marches across the Bug River into the Soviet breadbasket!" Without pause, Winchell jumped from reporting to commentary: "The Hun and his Nazi princes want to feed their war machine with Russian oil and wheat!"

Edna's father, Frank, looked at his wife, Sofya, and said, gravely, "Hitler won't stop unless somebody stops him."

Edna's mother, like Joseph Stalin, could not believe the news of the invasion and said, "I hope this is nothing more than a dreadful error."

Sofya was born in Zagorsk, Russia, a village near Moscow, and had immigrated to Milwaukee with her parents when she was five years old. She remembered enough Russian from her girlhood to speak with the *babushkas*, the old, thick-bodied Russian women with kerchiefs pulled tight around their heads whom she met on the street or at church.

Edna lifted her eyes and looked out the window, beyond the houses and trees to the blackened smokestacks rising like flagpoles above Cream City Steel, Milwaukee's only steel mill. At Cream City Steel, ingots were heated, shaped, cooled, and cut into half-inch-thick plates. The steel plates were loaded by crane onto flatbed rail cars and sent to Atlantic Coast shipyards to become the building blocks of American destroyers, cruisers, and troop ships.

Today, furnace smoke billowed and plumed out of the mill stacks, rose, broke apart, and disappeared into the pale blue sky. Edna exchanged the butter knife for a serrated bread knife and sawed a half-inch-thick slice off the five-pound baloney roll.

At seven-thirty, just as Edna was wrapping a piece of cake with wax paper, her father walked into the kitchen and said, "Let's go." Ever since Edna was old enough to find her way home on her own, she had walked her father partway to the mill, carrying his steel lunch box, eager to hear his work stories. He worked as a "heater" in the eighty-four-inch mill, heating steel ingots in an open hearth furnace. His work clothes stunk of raw steel and sweat.

Frank Vogt had grown up in Door County, outside the town of Sister Bay, on the pig farm his father had inherited from *his* father, who had immigrated from Germany before the turn of the century. Frank had graduated from the eighth grade, helped to bring the family herd up to fifty breeding sows, and then, the day he turned eighteen, had declared to his parents at the dinner table, "There's nothing more for me up here. I'm moving to Milwaukee. I'll get some new work. Look for a wife."

Edna and her father walked down the stairs of their upper flat, down the brick path laid from front porch to sidewalk, and onto the 34th Street sidewalk. Square, green lawns no larger than Edna's bedroom separated the sidewalk from the front-room windows of each two-family flat. Edna's father was quieter than usual.

"Do you think we'll go to war now?" she asked.

He pressed his lips together, shook his head, and said, firmly, as if to convince himself and her, "Ain't our war." Looking down, he kicked a jagged stone off the sidewalk, and added, "But if nobody stops Hitler ..." He didn't finished his sentence. Hitler's *Blitzkrieg*, or Lightning-War, had already defeated Czechoslovakia, Poland, Norway, Finland, the Low Countries, and France. Now, turning east, Hitler had invaded his ally, the Ukraine, surprising the whole world.

Without speaking, Edna and her father walked south on 34th Street. They watched a pair of gray squirrels chase each other around the trunk of a sidewalk elm. A bit further, they walked past a man sitting on his front steps, pulling on his work boots. He looked up, nodded to her father, and said, "Whoever said this was going to be a short war had his head up his rear end!"

"Don't look good, does it?" her father answered.

Ten minutes later, father and daughter headed down the wooded hill which divided their neighborhood from the industrial valley, a stretch of low land along the Menomonee River given over to train tracks and manufacturing plants like Falk, Harnishfeger, and Cream City Steel. This was where Edna usually said goodbye to her father, but not yet ready to part with him, she asked, "Can I walk you to the gate?"

He thought for a second and nodded.

At the bottom of the hill, they crossed Canal Street and three sets of train tracks, and came alongside the mill property fence. The chain-link fence surrounded five buildings, each with tall, filthy windows and walls of cream-colored brick blotched with black stains. They paused at the mill gate and turned toward each other. Edna handed her father his lunch pail and said, "Baloney on potato bread. Dill pickles. Angel-food cake."

He took the pail, smiled, bent toward her, and kissed her on the cheek, which provoked a cat-call and whistles from five young men coming up behind them. Her father turned to them and said, "A little respect for my daughter."

Edna watched her father join the men and walk shoulder to shoulder with them to the gate, where each held up his stamped steel badge to the guard. One young man with a blond crewcut and blue eyes turned around, looked Edna over from head to foot, and smiled. She looked away but was glad he had noticed her.

On her way home, Edna began to think again about what she was going to do with her life. She had never had a steady boyfriend, so becoming a wife and mother was beyond imagining. She had done well in school and liked learning, but she thought college was for other people – like her friend, Josie, who had grown up in a home with a baby grand piano in the living room and dark oil paintings in gold frames on the walls.

Edna knew that she had to get a job and start paying rent to her folks, which was fine with her. She wasn't interested in the kinds of jobs her girlfriends were getting – clerking, typing, filing – going to work each day in a dress, nylons, and high-heels, with curled hair, face makeup, fingernail polish, and perfume dabbed in the hollow of the neck and on each shoulder. Edna had once told her mother, "Women's work is just busywork, work the men won't do."

For the moment, Edna let herself dream, and her dream carried her back to the mill. At the mill, work was dangerous. Two years ago, she had heard her father sobbing in the kitchen, telling her mother about a co-worker who was cut in two by a body-length blade. At the mill, work was precise. Measurements were taken with a micrometer, in thousandths of an inch. At the mill, work was crucial to the country. Her father had once told her, "Each time I bring an ingot out of the furnace, Hitler's knees shake a little." At the mill, Milwaukeeans worked side by side: Poles and Mexicans from the South Side, Germans from the Near North Side, Russians and Serbs from Bay View, Negroes from downtown – all Americans, all men, except for the women who typed, filed, and clerked in the office.

At home, Edna found her mother in the backyard on her bare knees, picking tomatoes in the vegetable garden. Her mother looked up and said, "Betsy phoned for you. Said Schmidt is hiring at his bakery."

Edna nodded and said, "Might not be a bad place to work."

Edna liked to bake. She and her mother baked their own bread, rolls, cakes, and cookies. Edna got down on her knees alongside her mother, brushed her hand along a row of bean plants for a quick survey of the crop, and said, "Looks like we'll have enough for dinner." Her hands dove into the plants, searching, snipping, gathering the longest, thickest beans. Every once in a while, she glanced up at her mother, finally asking, "Are you thinking about ...?"

"Yes."

At noon, Edna joined her mother by the front-room radio and listened to the midday news. After reporting on the German advance into Russia, Walter Winchell added his commentary, "Now, it's Hitler against Stalin, Fascist against Communist, Nazi against Bolshevik, the Fatherland against Mother Russia!"

After lunch, Edna walked north on 34th Street to Michigan Avenue, a bustling business corner. She could smell the bread and rolls baking at Schmidt's Bakery. Edna turned east on Michigan, walked past the drug store which Josie's father owned and entered the open bakery door. Betsy, dressed head to toe in white, escorted her to the back room, where the mixing, stirring, kneading, rolling, frosting, and baking took place.

Betsy introduced Edna to the bakery owner, Elmer Schmidt, a man who had fled Germany and immigrated to America after the First World War. Edna glanced at his huge belly and wondered if he had to turn it sideways to get through a door. His head was bald and his face was round, with a striking white mustache which curved around his mouth like ivory tusks. Edna thought, he looks like a walrus!

Elmer Schmidt stood in front of a red-brick oven the size of a large backyard shed, with a narrow opening at eye level the width of the oven. Inside, she could see loaves of bread sitting on a floor of bricks, browning.

Elmer could see that his oven interested Edna, so he told her how he had built it from brick and sand, and how it held the heat for days. His *v*'s sounded like *w*'s, his *t*'s sounded like *z*'s, and his *r*'s gurgled from the back of his throat. She disliked his thick accent and walrus-body, but she needed a job and he offered one: "You vant to verk here?"

"What would I do?"

"Serve my customers, like Miss Betsy."

"Would I have to dress like her?" she asked.

"You no like vhite?" he asked, pointing to the white apron which stretched across his stomach.

"White is for nurses and brides," she replied.

He laughed, admiring her spunk.

"Can I work back here, near the oven? My dad works near a big oven – a furnace at the mill."

"You bake a little?"

"Rolls, biscuits, buns, cakes, and cookies!"

"Good! I let you bake vith me."

"How much will I make?"

He lifted his hands and held up seven fingers.

She nodded. Seven hundred dollars was a good yearly wage for a woman just starting out in 1941, a hundred more than she had expected. "What do I have to wear?"

"Vhite apron, like me."

The next morning, Edna began her new routine. She got up at four, an hour before her father, dressed in dark slacks and blouse, poured and drank a tall glass of milk, made her father's lunch, and stepped onto the dark porch, careful not to let the screen door slam behind her. The neighborhood was without sound, movement, or light. Ha! she thought. I'm up before the robins! Before the pigeons! Before the mill workers!

Ten minutes later, she stood in front of a steel table, pounding, folding, and punching a wad of bread-flesh, wearing an unstained, white apron, listening to Mr. Schmidt's countertop radio which he kept on each morning, at least until his first customer arrived.

At 5:00 a.m.: "Good morning, Mr. and Mrs. America and all the ships at sea. Today is July 9th, 1941. This is Walter Winchell reporting from New York." Winchell paused for a moment, then let his listeners hear a recording of Hitler's stirring, frenzied voice, referring again and again to *Das Dritte Reich*. A Nazi crowd chanted in the background, urging him on as if he were their preacher, and they, his choir.

"*Faschist!*" shouted Mr. Schmidt, startling Edna, letting her know in no uncertain terms that though he was from Germany, he hated Hitler. He walked to the radio, shut off Hitler's voice, turned to Edna, and said, "Hitler calls himself a Socialist, but he lies. He is a Faschist. A Faschist devil! *Der Teufel mit Schnurrbart,*" pointing to his own mustache with one finger.

"What does *Dritte Reich* mean?" Edna asked.

"Third Empire!"

Edna shook her head, still puzzled by the expression, so he explained it further: "Greece! Rome! Now Berlin! Each rules za earth for a tausend years!"

Edna scrunched her eyebrows. "Hitler wants to rule the earth?"

Mr. Schmidt stared at his new employee, amazed at her naiveté about the short, black-haired Bavarian who was the architect of the Third Reich.

"Miss Edna," Mr. Schmidt began. "The Nazi crowds sing, '*Deutschland, Deutschland, über alles,*' which means Germany over all za vorld!"

Edna was glad that Mr. Schmidt kept his radio on early each morning so that she could hear Winchell's reports on the war in Europe as well as Mr. Schmidt's commentary whenever Winchell broadcast Hitler's voice. On Monday, July 21st, she and her boss listened to Walter Winchell sign in and declare:

"Flash! – British intelligence reports that the Russian city of Minsk has fallen, and the Red Army has lost 3,785 tanks trying to defend her. Soviet T-34s are no match for Hitler's Panzer tanks, which can travel at forty miles an hour, and are now on their way to Kiev."

Edna shuddered at Winchell's words, imagining columns of Panzer tanks rumbling as fast as cars across the Ukrainian wheatfields, with black swastikas on white circles painted across their cannon turrets. Edna looked at Mr. Schmidt and said, "My mother will not take this news well. Her father was born in Kiev."

Not long after Winchell's report, Sofya phoned her daughter at the bakery and said, "Hitler is heading for Kiev! We must tell your grandfather. I'll come by the bakery for you."

At one o'clock, Edna took off her apron, now splotched with lard and butter stains, hung it from a hook on the brick oven wall, and walked into the bakery's front room, where her mother and Mr. Schmidt were speaking. Mr. Schmidt was saying, "Hitler has slit his own wrists by marching into the country of your father."

Her mother, surprised, asked, "Why do you say that? Nobody

has been able to stand against Hitler."

"Hitler now has two fronts! Sooner or later, he will bleed from each one."

Edna and her mother took the streetcar to Wanderer's Rest Cemetery. They walked around granite headstones shaded by drooping elm trees until they stood in front of a headstone, etched *"Serebna."* Edna's mother pursed her lips and shook her head, the summer breeze pressing her bangs across her forehead. Tears, perfect pools of grief, bulged in her eyes and slid down either side of her nose and around her quivering lips. Though Sofya said nothing, Edna had a sense that her mother, standing in the wind and sun, was speaking to her father, Vlas Markov Serebna, lying six feet under her.

Back on the streetcar, Edna asked her mother, "Did you tell him?"

"Yes."

"What did he say?"

She looked at her daughter's face, smiled, and yelled, "*Ourrah!*"

The other passengers turned toward Sofya, startled.

Edna frowned at her mother and asked, "What was that?"

"The Russian battle cry."

That evening at the dinner table, Edna told her father, "We visited Grandpa's grave today."

"Oh? Did you take flowers?"

"No. We took him the latest news," Edna said.

He nodded, looked at his wife, and said, "Too bad we can't put a radio on his headstone. He'd like Walter Winchell." Changing the subject, her father said, "They're adding a second shift at the mill. Supe said we got to get more Lend-Lease ships to the Allies."

Two days later, Edna and Elmer Schmidt paused from their baking and listened to Walter Winchell sign in and declare, with alarm, "Flash! – British Intelligence reports that German armor has captured Smolensk, less than two hundred miles from Moscow!"

Edna looked at her boss, who said, "Hitler tries to do vhat Napoleon could not do."

"What's that?" Edna asked.

"Take Moscow before Russian vinter!"

When Betsy arrived at six, Mr. Schmidt turned off the radio and waited to hear the jingling of the little bell tied to the door. He had the tradition of tending to the first customer of the morning himself. Edna had found out from Betsy that he used to speak German with most of his customers, but now no one who came into his store dared speak the language of Hitler in public.

On September 17, Edna, just home from the bakery, joined her mother by the front-room radio for the two o'clock news. Walter Winchell signed on and said, "The Ukrainian city of Kiev, along with dozens of Red Army divisions, is encircled by German artillery."

Sofya slammed her fist against the mahogany radio box, startling Edna. She looked into her mother's eyes, which flared with fury, as if she were seeing the German cannons and tanks coming straight at her. For a moment, Edna imagined her mother in Kiev, facing the Germans, in a Red Army uniform, lining up her rifle sights on a young German soldier.

As if building on Edna's fantasy, Walter Winchell added, "The Red Army, desperate for reinforcements, is now training women as pilots and snipers, and President Roosevelt declared that the

United States will send American Spam to the men and women of the Red Army."

The next morning, and the next, Edna's mother got up with Edna and both women stood alongside the front-room radio and listened to the 4:00 a.m. news out of New York. On September 19, Walter Winchell, in a tone far more subdued than usual, said, "British intelligence reports that Kiev has fallen, with the German army taking more than a half a million Red Army prisoners." In his commentary, Winchell directly addressed the President: "Mr. Roosevelt, sending American Spam to Russia will not stop Hitler and his Nazi princes. You must send American artillery and American boys in uniform!" Edna wished that America, like Russia, was recruiting women as snipers and pilots. Just maybe, she thought, I'd sign up.

After Winchell's report, Sofya turned and walked back to her bedroom. Edna followed and watched her mother get in bed without taking off her house dress, wiggle close to her sleeping husband, and pull their blue-and-purple patchwork quilt over her head.

In Milwaukee, October was warm and bright. The leaves on the street elms turned yellow gold, and the leaves on the park maples turned orange red. In Russia, October was cold and wet, the creeks swollen with brown, rushing water, the earth soaked to mud and slop. On October 2, the German armored commander, General Guderian, began his drive to Moscow, and it seemed to Hitler and the world that one final lunge would defeat Russia.

On Saturday morning, October 23, Frank left the house with his lunch pail for a day of overtime at the mill. Edna stood by the radio and her mother stood at the front-room window, watching

Frank walk down the street, both women listening for the news.

At eight o'clock, Walter Winchell said, "Good morning, Mr. and Mrs. America and all the ships at sea." In a cackly, excited voice, he continued: "Flash! – Russia's mud and snow have slowed the German drive to Moscow. Hitler now calls Russia 'the Swamp.' Russian T-34 tanks are built for swamp warfare! They're half-boat, half-tank!"

That evening, the wind and rain which had begun weeks ago in Russia came to Milwaukee, and by dark, trees bare of leaves stood out against the gray sky, the streets and lawns covered with a carpet of bright leaves.

On Thanksgiving Day, Edna woke up at four, as usual, but the house was not quiet. Her mother was in the kitchen, opening and closing cupboard doors, singing to herself. Edna dressed quickly and came down the stairs, expecting to find her mother salting and buttering a bare turkey carcass, but instead, she found her mother placing cubes of pale yellow pineapple across a loaf of bright pink meat. Seeing her daughter's surprise, Sofya said, "This Thanksgiving, we eat Spam, like the troops."

As soon as it got light, Edna noticed snow flurries in the air, drifting to earth, the first of the season. Just before eight o'clock, there was an unexpected knock at the front door, and Edna's mother said, "Oh my! Who could that be this early? Edna, see who it is."

Edna opened the door, startled to see her boss on the doorstep, bundled up in a long, black coat.

"Good morning, Miss Edna. Is your mother home?"

"Ma!"

Sofya appeared alongside her daughter at the door, wiping her wet hands on her strawberry-print apron.

Mr. Schmidt held out a square white box to Sofya and said, "A little something from my bakery for your Thanksgiving table."

"Why, Mr. Schmidt – you shouldn't have!"

He looked at Edna's mother, smiled, and said, "Do not lose heart, Mrs. Sofya. Moscow vill not fall like Kiev. Moscow has never fallen. Alexander Nevsky beat back za Teutonic Knights. Dmitri Donski held off za Tartars. Suvorov and Kutuzov battled off Napoleon. *Und* now, Zhukov will fight off Hitler, because the greatest Russian general of all time is on Russia's side!" Mr. Schmidt looked up at the gray mat of clouds across the sky and held out his hand. A single snowflake fell into his open palm.

Edna, astonished by her boss, asked, "Which general is that?"

Her mother smiled and said, "General Winter, dear. General Winter."

The Monday following Thanksgiving, Edna was back at the bakery, mixing dough, listening to the radio, while Mr. Schmidt, using a long-handled scoop, shoveled loaves of unbaked rye bread into the oven.

On the hour: "Good morning, Mr. and Mrs. America and all the ships at sea. This is Walter Winchell, reporting from New York. Today is November 27th, 1941. While Americans enjoyed the Thanksgiving holiday, the war in Europe raged on. Flash! – British intelligence reports that the German Fourth Army has reached Krasnaya-Poliana, fourteen miles from Moscow, within sight of the Kremlin towers on Red Square."

"You hear that, Mr. Schmidt?"

"Yes, Miss Edna."

"You still say Moscow will never fall?"

"Hitler needs to get his big guns ten miles closer to Moscow. Zat will be a long, cold ten miles for the Nazis, vith Russian soldiers behind every tree."

"How do you know?"

He paused for a long while before answering. "I grew up in Germany. And just like now, Germany and Russia fought. I fought za Russians."

She looked at her boss, imagining him as a young, slender soldier in German uniform, marching through the Russian forest, his eyes full of fear, certain that an infantryman was going to step from behind a tree at any moment and shoot him in the face.

On December 1st, the German Fourth Army made a final push to take Moscow and broke through the Russian lines at two points, but General Zhukov ordered every available soldier into the breaches and stopped the German advance.

Four days later, on Friday, December 5th, Elmer Schmidt and Edna listened to Walter Winchell: "Today, in Moscow, it is twenty below zero. Today, at dawn, Moscow time, the Red Army began a counter-offensive against the Germans."

Mr. Schmidt turned to Edna and said, "Tventy below is good fighting veather for Russians."

That evening at the dinner table, Sofya, so heartened by the news from Russia, declared, "We will go to church as a family this Sunday and give thanks to God."

The family used their black 1939 Plymouth on weekends and for special occasions. Frank, the only family member with a driver's license, brushed a light dusting of snow off the windshield, got in behind the steering wheel, and began the Plymouth's startup ritual – key, clutch, neutral, choke out, ignition. The V6 coughed, fired, caught, and belched a cloud of exhaust out the tailpipe. Choke in. Frank shivered. Heat out. He also turned on the car radio, spinning the radio dial, searching for news but hearing only choirs and preachers.

When the cab was warm, he tapped the horn, and his wife and daughter came out the back door. Sofya wore a maroon wool coat, with long black gloves, black high-heels and nylons, black dress, and a black cloth hat with face net, her dressiest outfit for funerals and church. The women joined Frank on the high, spongy bench seat of the Plymouth, and he backed out of the driveway and drove slowly down 34th Street.

Edna and Sofya got out of the car in front of St. Vladimir's Holy Russian Orthodox Church on Mitchell Street, and Frank drove off to park on a nearby frozen dirt playground owned by the Russian School of Milwaukee. The women turned and admired the church building, which they had not entered together for several years.

The church looked like it belonged in another world, another time. The building was built of brick as black as coal, startling in its contrast with the cream-colored brick which dominated the surrounding buildings. The church roof: five gold-leafed domes, one at the center, one on each corner, reflected the winter sun but looked as if they might be small suns themselves, glowing from within. The brick front was broken only by windows as tall and narrow as a tree trunk and two tall, slender doors of oak. The doors were cracked open just wide enough to allow in the young families and widows, one by one, as if someone were counting. Edna could see candle flames flickering inside the sanctuary.

Frank joined them on the sidewalk, and Sofya led her family

up the seven stone steps, between the doors, and into the sanctuary. Edna coughed as soon as she took a breath, the air heavy, smoky, and sweet from burning incense. The walls, painted a deep, rich red, were covered by icons – Byzantine paintings which featured stylized saints. The saints wore red, green, and black robes, their ashen, flat faces encircled by golden halos, like hoods. Their purpose: to provoke faith.

Worshippers did not sit, but rather stood, in family groups or alone, breaking away to light a candle or gaze at an icon. Sofya genuflected, and after making the sign of the cross, ended in the Russian way, with a bow. She led her family across the hard, shiny floor to a place near the icon of St. George, a Russian saint seated on a white horse, plunging his long spear into the black body of a coiled dragon. The image inspired Sofya, who thought of St. George as Russia and the coiled, black dragon as Nazi Germany.

The choir began singing from a loft behind and above the people, their music settling upon the people from above. Edna turned and studied the singers, who sang in Russian four-part harmony, without scores or accompaniment. The deep, forlorn voices of the basses made her shiver again, and she searched the faces of the basses until her gaze settled on a handsome young man, who returned her look as he sang. That's the guy I saw at the mill gate! she thought. He's looking right at me! This time, she smiled.

Edna's mother, gazing directly into eyes of St. George, felt hope and gratitude rise in her like incense smoke. Edna's father, a Lutheran, restlessly shifted his weight from one leg to the other. Like any Lutheran, he wanted to sit for worship.

The priests entered from the rear, the crowd parting to make way for their bearded, richly-robed clergy. The lead priest, dressed in a floor-length black robe and tall, black hat, swung a golden incense urn, from which rose clouds of rich smoke and odors. The second priest, also in black, held a gold-bound Bible above his head with his bare, white hands. The last priest, a bishop, wore a purple robe and carried a golden mitre. He held out his free hand for people to kiss as he passed them. Edna ignored the priests, keeping her eyes on the blond bass in the choir.

After worship, the family walked to the parking lot at the Russian School, which Sofya had attended as a girl. They got in their Plymouth, and Frank got the car going and turned on the radio and heat. A triple tone sounded on the radio, and the family was surprised to hear Walter Winchell, who did not usually broadcast on weekends:

"Good morning, Mr. and Mrs. America and all the ships at sea. This is Walter Winchell, in a special report from New York. Today is Sunday, December 7th, a day you will remember the rest of your lives! Flash! – the Imperial Navy of Japan has led a surprise attack on the U.S. Navy base in Pearl Harbor, Hawaii. Damage and loss of life is extensive. President Roosevelt issued a statement which called the attack 'devastating, ruthless, and cowardly.' He has asked Congress to convene in emergency session tomorrow, at 9:00 a.m., Washington time."

Winchell slapped his palm against his studio microphone, which sounded like an explosion, startling Frank, Sofya, Edna, and all his listeners. In a voice which no longer concealed his outrage, he added, "Those Japs won't ever surprise us again! It's our turn to surprise them!"

"We'll slaughter them!" Edna shouted, Winchell's outrage

provoking her own.

Frank opened his car door, stood, faced the people on the sidewalk, and shouted: "Pearl Harbor's been attacked by the Jap Navy!" Everyone who heard what he said stopped and looked at him, bewildered.

One man shouted back, "Where are you getting this?"

"Car radio! Walter Winchell!"

A man seated in a parked car shouted from his open window, "I heard it too."

A woman on the street yelled, "Where is Pearl Harbor?"

Frank shouted, "In Hawaii somewhere." People on foot hurried off to their car or home, eager to get by a radio. Sofya dropped her head and closed her eyes.

On Thursday afternoon of that week, Edna bundled up, put on her galoshes, and walked down the sidewalk, which was covered with a dusting of snow and looked to her like the powdered sugar sprinkled across Mr. Schmidt's coffee cakes. She waited by the mill gate for her father, her warm breath creating little clouds of steam in front of her face. Much to her surprise, she watched a woman about her age replace the male guard at the gate. Edna walked up to the woman and asked, "How long have you worked here?"

"This is my second week. Ain't enough men to cover all the jobs."

"Where would I apply for a job?" Edna asked.

The woman pointed to a one-story brick building and said, "At the office." She handed Edna a visitor's pass and added, "You can make good money here."

"I can make Hitler's knees shake a little, too."

Wanting to be considered on her own merits, Edna did not mention to the slender man with white shirt and bow tie that her father worked at the mill. She filled out a two-page application and gave it back to him. He handed her a test booklet and said, with gravity, "If you don't know an answer, do not guess – just leave it blank and go on to the next question. Sit at one of those desks."

Edna worked her way through questions about dimension, velocity, mass, weight, order, and scale – fifty difficult questions. She shook her head often, skipping many. I'll fail for sure, she figured. The man took her test, reviewing her answers.

Edna cleared her throat and said, "Maybe that test doesn't show it, but I can learn anything I need to know."

The man looked into her eyes.

She added, "If you hire me, you won't be sorry."

Her pluck inspired his trust. "Miss Vogt, when can you start?"

"Monday."

The man nodded. "First shift. Be right here at eight. You'll work in the 120-inch mill." He told her a few more details about her new job and handed her a plate of steel small enough to fit in a pocket, with her number – 1779 – stamped into each side. "That's your badge," he added. "Show it at the gate and whenever asked."

"What should I wear?"

He smiled and said, "Old clothes. Tough shoes." She walked home alone, gripping the badge in her hand like a silver dollar.

That night at dinner, Edna set down her fork, looked at her mother and father, and said, "I start a new job on Monday." They both stopped chewing and looked at her, waiting to hear more. "Twenty-three hundred, triple what I make at the bakery."

Her mother said, "Nonsense! Who's going to pay a young woman that kind of money?"

Edna reached into her pocket and set her Cream City Steel badge on the table as a centerpiece between their three plates. She looked at her father. "I didn't tell them you worked there. I got in on my own merits."

"The mill's no place for a young woman," Sofya said. "Frank, tell her." She stared at her husband, but he said nothing.

Sofya repeated, "Frank!"

"Used to be you was right, Sofya. But Pearl Harbor changed all that. Now, we got three shifts going, and the mill's been hiring women right and left.... Let Edna give it a try."

Sofya's eyes filled with tears. She set her fork and knife across her plate, stood, turned, and left the room, two slices of pot roast, a hill of peas, and a clump of mashed potatoes steaming on her plate.

Edna started to get up, but her father put his hand on her shoulder and said gently, "Let your mother have a little privacy. A job at the mill is not what she had in mind for you." He picked up his knife and fork and sliced a piece of roast on his plate, adding, "Fact is, I'm not sure I like you working there either. But it's wartime, and you ain't no schoolgirl any more."

The next morning, Edna arrived at the bakery, hung her coat on a wall hook, and put on her apron and hair net. At 5:00 a.m., she and her boss listened to the news:

"Good morning, Mr. and Mrs. America and all the ships at sea. This is Walter Winchell, reporting from New York. Today is December 14th, 1941. President Roosevelt told Congress that in order to mobilize for war, America will need to ration food, rubber, gas, and oil." Winchell's commentary: "That means every American man, woman, and child will get to play a part in defeating the evil powers intent on our destruction!"

After Winchell's report, Edna turned to her boss, who was standing by the oven with his back to her and said, "Mr. Schmidt. I've liked working here. You've been very kind to me."

He turned around.

"I got another job. Today is my last day here."

"Your new job is at za mill?"

"Yes."

He smiled at her like a father and said, "Hitler, Mussolini, and Tojo better vatch out now!"

On Wednesday morning, Edna got up and found her father busy in the kitchen, slicing inch-thick pieces of rye bread off a loaf from Schmidt's bakery. He looked at her, shrugged his shoulders, and said, "If you can roll steel, I can make lunch."

Astonished, she sat at the table and watched him butter the dark bread. "Where's Ma?" she asked.

Without turning around, he answered, "Still in bed. She don't feel too good today."

At seven-thirty, Edna and her father stood alongside the front-room radio and listened to Walter Winchell, who signed in and said, "Today is December 15th, 1941. British intelligence reports that Stalin, no longer afraid of a Japanese attack from the West, has transferred fresh, well-armed, warmly-dressed troops from Siberia to Moscow. Hitler's Panzer divisions, demoralized and exhausted, are in full retreat." His commentary: "Take heart, America! Hitler's best troops are on the run!"

Frank said, "I must tell your mother." He dropped the knife

and walked down the hall to deliver the good news to his wife. A minute later, he came back into the kitchen and again picked up the knife.

Edna asked, "What did Ma say?"

She said, "Grandpa can come back to his grave and get some rest."

At the front hall closet, father and daughter dressed for the long walk to the mill. Frank put on a sweater and wool overcoat, which stunk of steel, sweat, and smoke. "Daughter," he said. "Your clothes will soon stink like mine. But remember – it's the smell of victory."

They walked shoulder to shoulder to the mill, and at the gate, Edna proudly showed her badge, number 1779, to the woman guard, who smiled and winked. Edna's dad turned to Edna, handed her a lunch pail, and said, "Rye bread and baloney. Pickles. Orange." They parted.

The man with the bow tie and white shirt handed Edna another form, which she filled out. "You're set," he said. "Head out that door and down the walkway until you're at Building Five, the finishing mill. Ask for Supervisor Zipse. Give him this."

She left the quiet office building and walked into the noisy steel yard, where the ground beneath her vibrated from rumbling furnaces and slow-moving freight trains. Edna walked alongside the cooling yard between the finishing mill and straightening mill. The yard was crisscrossed with overhead crane tracks and low tracks of steel rollers which moved the 120-inch steel plates through cooling, inspection, and turning.

Each plate weighed as much as their family Plymouth, and when one plate banged against another or was turned over by heavy mechanical lifters, Edna felt the impact in her body. Stopping, she watched a tall, big-shouldered man in T-shirt, pants, and leather gloves ride on top of one of the plates as if it were already a ship at sea, and he, a sailor aboard it. Heat waves rose from the plate, his feet protected from the hot steel by wooden clogs.

She felt a tap on her shoulder and turned around, startled to see a man with ebony skin, curly black hair, and brown eyes. "Can you tell me where to find Supervisor Zipse?" she asked.

"Look no more."

"Oh!"

"You surprised I'm colored?"

"Well, I ..."

"Wartime is full of surprises."

She handed Zipse the form and said, "Put me to work."

He glanced at it, looked up, pointed to the man whom Edna had been watching earlier, and said, "That's Inspector Jackson. Don't expect him to jump for joy when he sees you's a woman."

Zipse took Edna into the finishing mill, where the pungent odor and heat from the steel plates intensified, in spite of electric fans with eight-foot blades pulling fresh air into, through, and out of the building. She followed Zipse up a dozen metal stairs into his office, which had floor-to-ceiling windows for walls. Edna noticed a sign on his desk, with two arrows: *Berlin 2,250 miles. Tokyo 3,800 miles.*

He had her fill out a form, then asked, "You like horses?"

"Horses?" she asked, confused.

She followed him out of his office and down the stairs. They stopped in front of a three-walled room the size of a closet, with red and yellow arrows pointing to a gray switchbox inside the room. "See that red button?" he asked.

"Yes."

"Nobody touch that button but me."

"What does it do?"

"Shuts down the mill."

Zipse turned and pointed to a tall young man with a blond crewcut who stood by a row of black handles and looked out over the cooling yard through tall windows. "That's John Folov," Zipse said.

Edna thought, that's the guy who eyed me at the mill gate and from the choir loft! She watched his bare, strong arms flex and harden each time he pushed a black handle, which triggered one of the mechanical lifts in the cooling yard.

Zipse added, "He joined the Navy. You get his job."

"Who's going to train me?"

"He is."

"Great!" Turning from Folov to Zipse, she asked, "What's a horse?"

"Them big iron arms which flip the plates – at your command."

Edna got a week of training from John Folov. The two hit it off right away, joking and laughing during breaks. Neither mentioned their previous encounters, but it was clear to each of them that the other remembered and cherished those moments. The first time Folov put his hands over Edna's hands on the black handles, an electric current passed between them which made Edna gasp. When he put his strong hands on her shoulders to adjust her position, she stopped breathing.

Twice, Folov got in an argument with Jackson, and after each argument, Folov told Edna, "Watch out for him – he's trouble."

Friday was Folov's last day at the mill. Just before lunch, he and Edna walked past the little room with the red button which shut down the whole mill. He took her hand and pulled her into the room, grabbed her by the hips, pulled her to him, and kissed her forehead. She reached behind his head and pulled his mouth to hers, moaning.

After a long kiss, he pulled back, looked into her eyes, unbuttoned her top shirt button, gently spread her shirt collar, and kissed her open neck. She did not resist. In fact, she pressed her chest against him, sure that he could feel her heart beating with his lips. The lunch whistle blew, startling them, and they pulled apart.

"If I write you, will you write back?" he asked.

"You kissed me, and I kissed back."

After lunch, Zipse approached Edna and said, "I got to borrow Folov. You're on your own for a bit."

Edna, on the job for the first time without assistance, stood in front of the black handles which controlled the mechanical horses and waited for the work whistle, nervous. Oscar Jackson, a silver and black coffee pot in one hand, walked past Edna. Seeing that she was alone, he paused, raised a finger, and said, "One mistake on your part and my wife will be a widow. You got that?"

"Yes."

"And don't Never, Never, flip a plate before you see my signal. Did Folov make that clear to you?"

"Yes."

Jackson walked into the cooling yard, climbed onto a plate, poured himself a cup of coffee, and set the pot on the plate beside him. The whistle blew. The cranes began moving and the plates began rolling. Jackson bent over and inspected the plate under his clogs, which took less than a minute. Taking his coffee pot, Jackson jumped to the next plate, looked at Edna, and raised his arm above his head, his signal that she could now flip the plate.

Edna grabbed the black handle to her left and pushed, which triggered a horse. The horse rose, and as it rose, the plate tilted and flipped over with a "*Boom!*" She flinched at the violent sound but thought with joy, I'm rolling steel!

Ten plates later, Edna watched Jackson grab his coffee pot and jump to the next plate. He set the coffee pot on the plate underneath him, turned around, looked at Edna, and raised his arm above his head. Edna nodded and pushed a black handle just as Oscar Jackson – for some reason unknown to Edna – jumped back on the plate which she was flipping.

"Oh my God!" she said. The horse rose beneath Jackson's clogs, tilting the plate. Jackson looked at Edna and waved both arms in panic – but there was no way to halt the horse once it began lifting the plate. Time shifted for Edna, as if she were watching the scene develop in slow-motion. Jackson, along with his empty coffee cup, began sliding toward the rollers. He squatted down and grabbed the rising edge of the plate with both leather-gloved hands, and looked straight up into the sky, hoping for a miracle from above. Edna thought, what have I done? He's going to be crushed by that plate and there's no way to stop it now! Her mind cleared for a moment: the red button!

Edna turned, dashed to the room where she had kissed John Folov before lunch, and slammed her open palm against the red button she was not supposed to touch. Lights, out. Cranes, fans, and rollers, stopped. The horse, which was about to flip the plate and make Oscar Jackson's wife a widow, halted.

Edna watched Jackson slide down the upended plate, jump off the rollers, and head for the building with huge strides. Her knees gave out, and she leaned against the wall and slid to the floor just as Jackson appeared above her, shouting and swearing, raising his arm as if to strike her. John Folov tackled Jackson from behind, and both men fell on top of Edna, grunting, shouting, kicking, and punching.

Zipse arrived and shouted, "Break it up!"

The men stopped fighting, rolled off Edna, and stood, breathing like winded animals. Edna got on her feet, slowly.

Zipse, his eyes and voice full of alarm, shouted, "What's going on here?"

All three of his workers began to reply at once.

"Hold it!" Zipse shouted. Pointing at Jackson, he said, "Wait for me outside." To Folov: "Wait for me in my office." To Edna: "Wait for me in the lunch room."

Edna walked across the mill floor, passing men who stood in bunches, watching her, talking, trying to learn from one another what had caused the unexpected shutdown and the floor fight. She sat in the empty, dark lunchroom, raised a cup of steaming coffee to her trembling lips, and took a tiny sip, just as the lights and fans came back on.

The lunchroom radio came back on and sounded the 10:00 tone, followed by: "Good morning, Mr. and Mrs. America and all the ships at sea. This is Walter Winchell, reporting from New York. Today is December 21st, 1941. Americans are preparing for war and for Christmas.

"Last night, our First Lady, Eleanor Roosevelt, lit the twelve thousand white lights on our nation's Christmas tree at Rockefeller Square. President Roosevelt declared from the White House that American shipyards are turning out an average of two warships every day for the United States Navy." He paused, adding: "There's nothing America can't do when she sets her mind to it!"

Zipse entered the lunchroom with Jackson's coffee pot, turned off the radio, and sat across the polished steel table from Edna.

"I shut down the mill," she said.

"Folov and Jackson told me. Jackson said you lifted a plate before his signal."

An anger rose in her like heat through steel, and she pounded the table with her fist, startling her supervisor, splashing hot coffee out of her cup and across the table. "That's either an outright lie or he's got steel for brains!" she said. "He jumped to a new plate, gave me his signal, and then for some reason, he turned around and jumped back onto the plate I was lifting! If I hadn't shut down the mill, he'd be dead."

"I fired him," Zipse said.

Her anger gave way to surprise and alarm, certain now that she too would be fired. "Just because he made a mistake?" she asked.

"No. Because he was drunk."

"Drunk?"

Zipse slid Jackson's coffee pot across the table to Edna and said, "Take a whiff."

She bent down and sniffed the coffee spout, whiskey stink stinging her nostrils. Looking at Zipse, she asked, "You got to fire me now, don't you?"

"Why?" he asked, surprised. "You been sipping Jackson's coffee?"

"I pushed the button you told me not to touch."

Zipse reached across the table, put his dark, warm hands around her cold, pale hands and said, "I can't fire you for thinking quick. You saved a man's life." Standing, he added, "Finish your coffee and get back to your horses. We got a war to win."

Ten minutes later, Edna walked out of the lunchroom and back to the black handles at her work station. John Folov was waiting for her and said, "Zipse said you're ready to work alone. I'll be inspecting the plates in the yard. Let's use the same signal."

She put her hands on the black handles, and he could see her hands tremble, so he put his hands around hers. "You alright?"

"I'm just shook up. I'll be fine."

After her shift, Edna met her dad at the mill gate, and the two walked home, side by side. When her father spoke of the unexpected shutdown just after lunch, she said nothing, not yet sure how to speak of the incident to him, let alone her mother.

At home, Edna found her mother in the kitchen, spreading chocolate frosting on a white angel-food cake. Sofya looked up and said, "Get out of those clothes and help me in the kitchen. I met Elmer Schmidt today and he's coming for dinner – wants to know all about your work at the mill." She stepped back, tilted her head, studied her cake, and asked, "Think he'll like my cake?"

"He'll want your recipe!" Edna said, adding, "I got someone coming for dinner too – John Folov, a new friend from work."

"Oh! A young man?"

Edna nodded.

"With a Russian name, no less!" Sofya said happily.

The sun set on the shortest day of the year, and the two women stood side by side at the sink, peeling carrots and potatoes, speaking about when to put up the Christmas tree. Edna glanced up often, looking out the window above the sink, past the bare back-yard maple and across the expanse of the industrial valley, which was already in deep shadow.

She could see white smoke pouring into the darkening sky from a tall smokestack, and she thought, I'll work at the mill until the war is over – then I'll go to college. This thought surprised and delighted her. College was no longer just for other people. She imagined herself walking down 34th Street toward Marquette University, a stack of hardcover books pressed against her breasts.

At the dinner table, Frank said, "Let us pray.... Dear God. We thank you for our daily bread and for all our blessings. Amen." Sofya crossed herself in the Russian way, noticing that John Folov did the same. As Sofya began passing the platters of roast, mashed potatoes, and carrots, John and Edna glanced at each other, smil-ing but saying little. Frank and Sofya kept an eye on the looks between their daughter and the young man.

Mr. Schmidt did most of the talking, speaking about the bakery, the winter, the roast. After plopping a mountain of mashed potatoes on his plate, he turned to Edna and asked, "How vas your day at za mill, Edna?"

Edna glanced at her former boss, her mother, her father, and John Folov, who winked at her as she considered her answer. Edna said, "Had a good day. Rolled some steel. Got kissed by a young man. Shut down the mill to save a man's life. The usual."

Sofya glanced at John Folov, looked at her daughter, and said, "You got kissed at the mill?"

John Folov squinted, frowned, and said, "If I ever get my hands on the guy that did that, I'll fix him good!"

Frank stared at his daughter, his forkful of carrots brought to a standstill halfway between his dinner plate and his mouth. "*You* shut down the mill?" he asked.

Mr. Schmidt chuckled and said, "Tomorrow morning, I vill turn on za radio and Valter Vinchell vill say, 'Flash! - Edna Vogt has got za Axis Powers on za run!'"

BLESS EWE

THE BARN WAS QUIET, as if empty of animals, until the first sheep heard our boots crunch the frozen dirt as we approached the door.

"*Baaaa!*" A sheep solo.

Grandpa opened the barn door, and the sheep jerked their white faces toward us, opened their mouths, curled their pink tongues over their yellow teeth, and bleated.

"*Baaaa! Baaaa! Baaaa!*" A sheep chorus.

I stepped out of the cold, brittle air and into the sheep-warmed, manure-sweetened air, grabbed a pitchfork, and threw some loose hay into one of the wooden mangers. The ewes broke for the manger like kids, shoving, butting, and squirming. Butch, the black-faced ram, paced back and forth in his separate corral, unable to reach his ewes or that first pitchfork of hay.

Grandpa, the shepherd, and I, his sixteen-year-old Christmas-break assistant, filled each manger with dry timothy and alfalfa. The sheep surrounded the mangers, shoved their heads between the wooden slats, and muscled in up to their wooly shoulders. Each sheep fell silent with its first mouthful of hay, until the barn was again quiet, except for the heavy breathing and munching of forty Suffolks.

Butch ate in his own manger but did not like his separate quarters or special treatment. He wanted to be with his girls, protecting, nuzzling, and mounting each and every one as often as possible – monogamy had never taken hold in the barn.

We watched the sheep feed. Grandpa said, "Next week, I'll let Butch in with his ewes." This meant that by late winter, the ewes would be lambing, the first sign of spring in a land where ice and snow stuck around until Easter. During lambing, Grandpa stayed in the barn day and night, helping deliver Butch's offspring. A large white-faced ewe, finished with her supper, backed away from her manger. Grandpa pointed at her and said, "She's more calm than most. Take her."

Grandpa left to ready the trailer, and I jumped into the sheep pen and swung my leg over the ewe's head. Straddling her neck, I guided her into the barnyard and through the gate. God, she's fat! I thought. When she saw the trailer, her eyes got big and her breath shot from flared nostrils in short bursts. "Don't look so worried," I said. "You're not going to market. You're going to Bethlehem."

In the car, I sat behind Grandma, the defroster blowing warm air and the odor of her talcum powder into the back seat. Grandpa drove fifteen or twenty miles an hour into town, the snow tires on his 1963 Nova crunching little pebbles of ice against the asphalt.

How odd that I am on my way to church, I thought. As a kid, I had happily gone to church with my parents. But when I hit my teens, I had to sit through weekly confirmation class with Reverend Klug, a meticulous, serious man who wore black from head to foot, with the exception of a white tab collar just below his bony adam's apple. He combed his white hair every fifteen minutes with a silver comb, raising his flattened pompadour from the dead. Reverend Klug never smiled, but he always knew what was good and right, and he taught us that the religious life was about learning and obeying the "Thou shalts" and "Thou shalt nots." Confirmation made me a church member but ruined my appetite for God, and I had not darkened a church door in four years.

I asked Grandpa, "Do you put one of your ewes in the Lord's service every Christmas?"

He glanced at me in the rearview mirror, put his eyes back on the road, and said. "No. This is the first time."

Grandma turned around and said, "Your grandfather couldn't say no to our new minister!"

"He's had a rough go so far, " Grandpa said.

"Why?" I asked, scarcely able to imagine a minister with troubles of his own.

"He's still wet behind the ears – could be your older brother," Grandpa said.

"Some think he's too cozy with the Catholics," Grandma said. In that town, Protestants were the sheep, and Catholics were the goats, and every farmer knew that the two didn't mix, but Grandma said that their new minister did not know this and did not want to learn it. After a moment, she added, "And he could use a wife."

Grandpa drove down Main Street, turned right at Fourth Street, and parked alongside the curb near the side entrance to the church. He turned to me and said, "Find the Reverend. Ask him where he wants to take delivery."

"How will I recognize him?" I asked.

"Black hair. Skinny. Tall," Grandpa said.

"He'll be wearing blue jeans," Grandma added. "That's part of his problem. He looks like he's ready to step into the barn, not the pulpit."

Maybe I'll like this guy, I thought.

In the social hall, I found a young man who fit the description, surrounded by two dozen young children. The man wore a baggy long-sleeved white shirt, open at the collar, and a pair of faded jeans. His black bangs covered most of his pale forehead. I liked him right away, probably for the same reason that his church folk disliked him – he seemed like a regular guy: bad haircut, awkward with kids, and worried, his eyebrows pulled together into a frown above his eyes, alert for what might go wrong. I thought, this guy knows he won't escape trouble just because he's got religion.

The girls, dressed as angels, wore white robes and gold-tinsel elastic headbands. The boys, dressed as shepherds, wore brown robes and carried sticks as staffs. The minister spoke to the children, "Find your Bethlehem Buddy!" While the children arranged themselves, he glanced up at me and asked, "Can I help you?"

"Otto Kepler, my grandfather, wants to know where you'd like to take delivery of the sheep."

"A real sheep?" asked a boy shepherd. The children quieted, studying me.

"Bring him here," said the minister.

"Her."

"Ah! Bring *her* here, quick! T-minus three minutes and counting."

Back at the trailer, I threw my leg over the ewe's neck, got her head between my legs, and guided her down the sidewalk and toward the side door of the church. Grandpa, the experienced farmer-shepherd, knew when to leave the work to his assistant. He and Grandma, skirting icy spots in the sidewalk, walked to the front of the church.

When the ewe and I walked into the social hall, there was a moment of silent reckoning between children and animal. The ewe, which had never seen the inside of any building except her barn and had never known that children traveled in herds, let out a "*Baaaaaaa!*" The boys raised their staffs above their heads like spears, ready to take charge of their new keep. The girls forgot their heavenly status and returned to earth, eager to help the humble shepherds with real work.

The ewe jerked her head out from between my legs, turned, and tried to run, but her hooves slipped on the polished maple floor, and she fell to her fat belly. The minister shouted, "No one move!" Every child bolted toward the ewe as she struggled to stand and they formed a perfect circle around her, each child's body a picket in a human fence. The ewe, eyes wild, peed onto the floor, which delighted the children.

One boy pointed at the splashing pee and yelled at the animal, "Hey, you can't do that. It's Christmas Eve!"

I looked and first noticed the ewe's bulging udder.

The minister walked up to me and said, "The children are a little surprised. I didn't tell them that a live sheep was part of the program."

"Did you warn the adults?"

"Nope," he said, smiling. "They've been surprising me since I came here. It's my turn to surprise them."

"Who's going to manage the ewe in church?"

"You."

"Me? I didn't sign up for this."

"I know. But would you do it?"

"I suppose." I couldn't say no to him either.

What's your name?" he asked.

"Jake."

The minister smiled and extended his hand. "Jake, I'm Steven Schneider, shepherd of the earthly flock which pastures here at St. Peter's." I shook his hand and thought, Wow! a minister with a first name and a sweaty palm. This guy is no Reverend Klug.

The children kept the ewe surrounded while Schneider helped me put on a long brown robe. He pulled a white robe, the color of clean sheep's wool, over his head and let it drop to his ankles like a dress. After tying a braided belt around his waist, he draped a golden stole across his shoulders. The stole hung to his kneecaps and glittered when it caught the light a certain way. Between the bottom of his robe and his shoes: three inches of faded jeans. Even in his robe, he looked ready for the barn.

Five minutes later, we gathered in the church narthex, a kind of holding pen for people near the sanctuary's entrance. Each child found his or her Bethlehem Buddy and lined up side by side. I stood across from Schneider, the ewe's head still between my legs, the bottom of my robe arching across her neck.

A barrel-chested man, dressed in a navy suit, stood in front of the closed sanctuary doors, his arms folded across his chest, his eyes on the ewe, bracing for trouble. He uncrossed his arms and held an erect finger to his arching lips, trying to shush the children. Schneider leaned toward me and said, "That's Jim Graf."

"He looks like a bouncer," I whispered.

"He's Head Usher," Schneider said. "But if he were a bouncer, I'd be his first bouncee."

"What's he got against you?" I asked.

"He says I'm too soft on the Communists and the Catholics." Schneider leaned closer to me and added, "He's not the only one who wants me out. This is my first Christmas in this church. And it might be my last."

His frank confession startled me. I wondered what advice Reverend Klug might give him: "No more smiling! Get a haircut and a silver comb!" I had no advice to give Schneider, but I began to hope that he would pull through his troubles and be around a long time.

Graf walked up to Schneider and asked, "What's that animal doing here?"

"She's got a non-speaking part tonight," said Schneider.

Graf turned to me and asked, "Who are you?"

"Otto Kepler's grandson."

Graf turned away, put his hands on the shoulders of a short, blonde angel, and bent down to whisper to her.

"That's Graf's youngest granddaughter, Emily." Schneider said. "I gave her a speaking part." The young minister looked worried whenever he glanced at his Head Usher, and now I knew why.

The organist hit her opening chord, and Graf swung open the doors, stooped down, and slipped a little triangle of wood under each door to hold them open. The sanctuary looked dark and bright at once, lit only by altar candles and tiny white lights strung around a Christmas tree near the pulpit. A few people turned around in their pews to get a look at the children, and the congregation began singing, from memory, "O come, all ye faithful, joyful and triumphant...."

Schneider walked by Graf, leaned into him, and said, "There's a yellow puddle on the social hall floor."

Graf looked at the ewe and frowned.

"Better there than on the carpet," Schneider added.

Two by two, the children followed their minister up the red aisle carpet on the long procession from narthex to chancel, from Nazareth to Bethlehem. The ewe and I brought up the rear. Reverend Schneider looked over his shoulder. He smiled at the paired angels just behind him and looked over the heads of the other angels and shepherds to see how the ewe was reacting to two hundred voices raised in song. No problem. The singing seemed to calm her.

"O come ye, O come ye to Bethlehem...." We were almost to Bethlehem, another fifty feet.

"Come and behold him, born the king of angels...." The words came back to me, and I sang too.

> *O come, let us adore him,*
> *O come, let us adore him,*
> *O come, let us adore him,*
> *Christ the —*

"*Baaaaaaaaaaa!* " The ewe's shrill bleat jolted the faithful, who had expected to hear *about* sheep but not *from* sheep that evening. I grabbed the ewe's muzzle and held her mouth shut. Schneider, already in his pulpit and facing his people, raised his face to the dark ceiling and laughed. I thought, he's enjoying his little surprise!

By the fourth verse of the carol, all of the angels were arranged around the pulpit, each standing on an X of masking tape stuck to the carpet, their open hands pressed together with fingertips pointing toward heaven. All of the shepherds, including me, were bunched together on our knees in front of the altar and behind the ewe, facing the congregation. I kept an arm across the ewe's neck and a hand across her muzzle. The organist ended the carol. The congregation sat and quieted, ready to hear the Christmas story told by the happy, little voices of those who still lived close to mystery.

Schneider, the narrator, began the gospel story from the pulpit microphone, using King James English:

"Now the birth of Jesus Christ was on this wise: When as his mother Mary was espoused to Joseph, before they came together, she was found to be with child of the Holy Ghost. Then Joseph, her husband, being a just man, and not willing to make her a public example, was minded to put her away privily. But while he thought on these things, behold, an angel of the Lord appeared unto him in a dream, saying ..."

Schneider paused and looked at the oldest angel. She stepped forward to the kid's microphone, gulped, concentrated, and then spoke:

"Joseph, thou son of David, fear not to take unto thee Mary thy wife; for that which is conceived in her is of the Holy Ghost. And she shall bring forth a son, and thou shalt call his name Jesus; for he shall save people from their sins."

The ewe twitched her head and snorted.

From the pulpit, Schneider read again – about taxes, about the journey to Bethlehem, about the birth of the holy child.

"... And Mary brought forth her firstborn son, and wrapped him in swaddling clothes, and laid him in a manger: because there was no room for them in the inn."

Schneider nodded at a boy shepherd, and the boy stepped forward to the microphone:

"And there were in the same country shepherds abiding in the field, keeping watch over their flock by night. And, lo, the angel of the Lord came upon them, and the glory of the Lord shone round about them: and they were sore afraid."

The shepherd rejoined his kind, and Graf's granddaughter, Emily, stepped to the microphone, cleared her throat, and said: "The angel said unto them –"

"*Baaaaa!*"

The girl lost her train of thought and fell silent as she – and all of us in that sanctuary – watched the ewe drop to her belly as if stricken. Oh God! I thought, she's going to die right here in front of God and half the folks in town.

The ewe laid her head on the red carpet and rolled to her side, the congregation now murmuring, the children staring. Thinking of Grandpa, Schneider called out, "Is there a shepherd in the house?"

Grandpa appeared from out of the dark sanctuary and knelt beside his ewe, looking at her eyes, one hand resting against her bulging side, one hand exploring her belly. I knelt next to him, and Schneider walked up behind me, looking down at the ewe, puzzled.

"Maybe she's sick," Schneider said.

"She ain't sick," Grandpa said. "She's lambing!"

The ewe stiffened her legs.

"She's what?" Schneider asked, incredulous.

"She's lambing!" Grandpa repeated, loud enough for all to hear. People gasped.

Graf, the Head Usher, came up behind Grandpa and took up a stance a few steps to the side, his face twitching, his body uncertain of his next move as guardian of the Order of Worship. Graf's granddaughter Emily bolted from the frightened angels to stand alongside him, wrapping her slender, pale arms around his thick leg.

Grandpa looked up at Schneider, a confounded look on his face, and said, "But this ewe ain't been bred, Reverend."

Another collective gasp from the congregation. The people had expected to hear *about* a virgin birth, not *see* one.

My first thought: Before we jump to conclusions, let's talk to Butch!

Graf, realizing he was up against more than disorder, blurted out, "What are we to make of this?"

Schneider looked up toward heaven, as if expecting a little guidance from his Boss.

"I feel the head," Grandpa said. "The head's coming first."

I cradled the ewe's heavy head in my lap. Her eyes rolled, her breath came coarse and quick, and her pink tongue hung out between her rows of yellow teeth and black gums.

"The head's out!" Grandpa said.

The ewe's stiffened legs trembled and her body convulsed once, twice, thrice, and squirted her lamb's slimy, still body into Grandpa's waiting hands. Another surprise: the lamb was black as the night sky, from its tiny, soft hooves to its folded, soaked ears.

"*Schwarzes Schaf*," Grandpa said – a black sheep. He took a white handkerchief from his suitcoat pocket and cleaned the lamb's face, his thumb thicker than the lamb's neck. He handed me, his assistant, the handkerchief, bent over, put his open mouth over his lamb's twitching nostrils, blew, and filled the little lungs with their first breath.

Surprising everyone, Grandpa gently picked up the lamb and offered it to Schneider, reminding the minister of his role as shepherd of the St. Peter's flock. Schneider glanced at Grandpa, nodded, took the little creature, and lifted it high above his head like a chalice. Next, he stepped off the chancel, walked past Jim Graf and down the center aisle, slowly, so that his people could see the little black creature which had just entered this world. People stood on tiptoe, eyes wide, mouths open, leaning to the right or left for a better look. No one said a word.

As if still following a rehearsed order, one boy-shepherd, along with his Bethlehem Buddy, stepped off the chancel and walked up behind Schneider, eager to provide backup. The rest of the boys followed, in pairs.

Emily Graf, not wanting to be left out of the procession, let go of her grandfather's leg, waved over *her* Bethlehem Buddy, and the two girls fell in behind the shepherds. They were quickly joined by the rest of the angels.

Schneider, nodding and smiling, glanced behind him at the children, happy they had joined him.

Graf, regaining his sense of tidiness, stared at the pool of pink afterbirth soaking into the carpet and muttered, to nobody in particular, "That stain will never come out."

The ewe rolled off her side and onto her belly, looking behind her, searching for her newborn.

"*Baaaa!*"

The shrill bleat of the ewe caused Schneider – and the children – to halt and turn around, reversing their procession, walking back toward the chancel. The angels couldn't have been happier, since the shepherds were now following them. Schneider, now at the rear of the procession, cradled the lamb against his chest like a newborn child and began to sing a Christmas lullaby as he processed. Everyone joined him, even old man Graf.

> *Silent night, holy night,*
> *All is calm, all is bright,*
> *Round yon virgin, mother and child,*
> *Holy infant, so tender and mild,*
> *Sleep in heavenly peace,*
> *Sleep in heavenly peace.*

By the end of the first verse, Schneider was again alongside Grandpa, and the shepherds and angels were again standing on their X's taped to the chancel carpet. Schneider gently set the lamb in front of the ewe. She smelled and nudged her newborn, pulling her thick, pink tongue across the dark, trembling body.

Someone in the congregation began singing "Away in a Manger," another Christmas lullaby, and we all sang along without taking our eyes off the ewe and her black lamb.

After a few more quiet carols, Schneider held up the printed Order of Worship and said, "Let's all sing the closing carol." The members of the congregation looked around and picked up the staple-bound booklets lying on the pews, nearly forgotten. Schneider turned to the organist, nodded, and she began playing.

I kept an eye on the ewe and her lamb as the congregation began to sing.

> *In the bleak midwinter, frosty wind made moan,*
> *Earth stood hard as iron, water like a stone.*
> *Snow had fallen – snow on snow, snow on snow,*
> *In the bleak midwinter, long ago.*
>
> *Angels and archangels may have gathered there,*
> *Cherubim and seraphim thronged the air.*
> *But his mother only, in her maiden bliss,*
> *Worshiped the beloved with a kiss.*
>
> *What can I give him, poor as I am?*
> *If I were a shepherd, I would bring a lamb.*
> *If I were a Wise Man, I would do my part.*
> *Yet what can I give him? Give my heart.*

After that carol, Schneider faced the ewe and her lamb, smiled, and said, "Bless you." Turning to the congregation, he raised his arms and said, "The earth is the Lord's, and the fullness thereof. Merry Christmas."

It was clear to everyone that he had just pronounced the benediction, and people turned to one another and began to visit, quietly. Parents left their pews and came to the chancel, getting a closer look at the ewe and her lamb as they gathered their boy-shepherds and girl-angels. Graf, his hand holding the hand of his granddaughter, chatted with Schneider and Grandpa.

When the sanctuary was nearly empty, Grandpa got his ewe back on her feet, and I picked up the lamb. Graf reappeared with a bucket of hot water and a towel, dropped to his knees, and began cleaning up the afterbirth.

Schneider reappeared too, having exchanged his white robe for a navy nylon parka, letting Grandpa and me know that he would help us take the ewe and her lamb back to the barn, where together the three of us would build a small corral, line it with fresh straw, move the ewe and her lamb into their new quarters, and have that talk with Butch.

COME ABOUT!

AFTER THE CIVIL WAR, the Great Lakes became the principal highways of commerce connecting the northern states. Sailing ships - scows, hookers, and three-masted schooners – carried lumber, ore, grain, machinery, and dry goods to and from busy ports up and down the lakes.

During the shipping season of 1880, favorable sailing weather lasted well into October, but on Friday, October 15th, the winds shifted and began to blow out of the southeast, gaining velocity all night. By Saturday morning, winds up to ninety miles per hour blew across the Great Lakes, accumulating their greatest fury over the length of Lake Michigan. This storm – the worst storm in the recorded history of the Great Lakes – damaged, stranded, and sunk dozens of ships in what became known as "The Big Blow of 1880."

The harsh cry of a gull broke the dawn silence of the Milwaukee harbor on Friday, October 15th, 1880. Long, thin clouds drifted across the sky like graceful white birds, their bellies pinkened by a sun still out of sight. Captain Theodore Lane, a slight man with black hair, black beard, and the bearing of a much older man, stood on the deck of the *Julia Hart*, preparing himself for the final voyage of the season.

For the past three days, stevedores had loaded the *Julia Hart* with four thousand barrels of salt and one spinet, all bound for Fish Creek, a Wisconsin village on Green Bay, where Lane planned to unload his cargo, winter his ship, and marry his beloved. He lit his black pipe, faced east, and squinted as the sun broke above Lake Michigan. The smoke from his pipe tobacco swirled, rose, and drifted off to the west, and the lake lapped against the two-inch-thick oak hull of his vessel like the steady breathing of a creature asleep.

Captain Lane's vessel, a three-masted schooner, measured one hundred and forty feet from stem to stern. It displaced two hundred tons without cargo, and could do fifteen knots under full sail with a crew of eight. Captain J.M. Valentine, Lane's predecessor, had made himself and the *Julia Hart* famous among Great Lakes sailors in 1877 by riding her over the Chicago breakwater on a huge wave during a big blow.

Two days after that incident, David Lawrence Hart, the owner of the *Julia Hart*, had dismissed Valentine on charges of "bravado and recklessness" and installed Lane as her Captain. Ship captains were confident men who loved adventure and risk, but on the Great Lakes – with life, property, and reputations at stake – they usually erred on the side of caution. A sailor's saying: "There are bold captains. There are old captains. But there are never old, bold captains."

Soren Torgeson, Lane's Chief Mate, stepped onto the deck of the *Julia Hart* from below, pulled his wool watch-cap over his blond hair, and walked toward Lane. Torgeson was a Swede from

Door County, a big man with good sailing instincts and a strength and quickness made legendary by his boxing victories at ports all across the Great Lakes. "Good morning, Captain," he said. "Do we sail today?"

"We do."

Torgeson checked the sky with a sailor's eye, and said, "Never have I seen such fine sailing weather this late in the season."

"Nor have I."

Earlier that season, the Federal Government had opened the first Weather Bureau on Lake Michigan, at the Sturgeon Bay Lighthouse. Ship captains took notice of the Bureau's forecasts, but like most sailors of the era, they trusted their own instincts more than any Bureau.

Captain Lane said, "I am puzzled as to why the Sturgeon Bay Bureau put up the storm flag two days ago." Lane had learned of the storm warning from a fellow captain who had sailed past Sturgeon Bay on his way to the Milwaukee harbor.

Torgeson chuckled. "The man running the Bureau is no sailor. His name is Increase Claflin. He learned his weather out of books."

"Prepare the ship for sea," Lane ordered.

"Aye, aye, sir."

"And send a lookout up the mast."

Lane watched one of his sailors climb the ratlines up the main mast, a single white-pine trunk nearly as long as the vessel. All three masts had been shaped, tapered, and oiled by skilled hands, lifted into place by a team of six black Percherons, and secured with rope riggings known as sheers. No sooner had the sailor reached the trestletree, fifty feet up the mast, than he pointed to the north and shouted, "Hart's carriage ahoy!"

The young captain walked down his vessel's gangway and met Hart's carriage. The driver swung off his high seat, jumped to the ground, opened the carriage door, and David Lawrence Hart, the owner of Lane's vessel, stepped onto the dock. He walked directly up to Lane and said, "I trust you will provide the best care for my daughter and her attendant, Captain Lane."

"Their comfort and safety are my highest concern."

Hart nodded.

Captain Lane's heart swelled when he saw his bride-to-be emerge from the carriage. She was dressed in an ankle-length black dress and a white, ruffled, high-collared blouse. Her auburn red hair was elegantly gathered and bound to the top of her head with long pins and a tiny black hat. Annie Marie smiled and offered one hand to her father and one hand to Lane. The men escorted her up the gangway, followed by the carriage driver and Annie Marie's attendant, a young, sturdy, unmarried maidservant named Maggie Clark. Annie Marie pointed at the intricate world of masts, spars, rigging, and shrouds and said, "It looks like a giant spider-web."

Annie Marie had often wanted to sail on one of her father's schooners, but her father had never allowed it. "That lake is no place for a young woman!" he had often said, an objection which she had accepted – until she began planning for her wedding.

On the fifth of August, Captain Lane had written to Annie Marie about his final voyage of the 1880 season, and she had chosen November first as her wedding date and the Fish Creek Captains' Club as her wedding site, an elegant wooden mansion for maritime officers. As an early wedding gift to the couple, Hart had rented a room in Fish Creek for their use that winter.

In the midst of preparing for her wedding, Annie Marie had startled her father by declaring, "I will sail to my wedding with my darling Captain."

"Don't talk such nonsense," her father had said. "I will escort you by train and carriage to Fish Creek, as planned." But Annie Marie, weary of a safe, proper life under the guidance of her father, ignored her father's objection.

On the tenth of August, Annie Marie had written Lane, "I will accompany you on your vessel from Milwaukee to Fish Creek. This is as it should be." Captain Lane had accepted her choice to accompany him as "the bride's prerogative," but privately he worried about a woman's comfort aboard a vessel built for cargo, not passengers. Most women of that day used passenger steamers for Great Lakes travel.

Lane led Hart and the women to his Captain's Quarters, a small, stout cabin built on the stern deck. He opened the door and said, "Ladies – my quarters are yours for this voyage. I will make my quarters below deck."

Annie Marie walked past him, noticing each sparse detail of the room: three small shuttered windows, two narrow bunks, table, writing desk, and for this trip, Annie Marie's spinet.

"Oh, Theodore – my spinet! I shall play for you and your crew this evening."

Hart looked at his daughter and said, "It is not too late to change your mind and travel with me by train. I leave this morning."

Annie Marie looked at him, offered him her hand, and said, "Goodbye, Father. I will see you in Fish Creek."

"Very well, daughter," he said, resigning himself to her decision. After tenderly kissing his daughter's hand, he turned to his carriage driver and said, "You may bring the luggage." Next, he turned to Captain Lane and said, "I shall personally inspect the seaworthiness of this vessel before I depart."

An hour later, the *Julia Hart* cleared the Milwaukee breakwater, with waves between two and three feet and winds between seven and ten knots, too light for making good time. Standing on the deck with Annie Marie, Lane said, "We'll go offshore two miles, then turn north towards our destination of Fish Creek, following the coast and keeping two miles off the headlands. We'll navigate by fixing our position against landmarks."

Annie Marie, her hands braced against the deck railing, studied the wooded shore, the sweep of green foliage interrupted here and there by a yellowing ash or reddening maple. Tall, brick estates stood atop Milwaukee's Lake Drive bluff like lighthouses. Annie Marie said, "The air is so fresh and pure! I love it out here! Can you see my father's home, Theodore?"

Lane pulled his brass telescope out of his pocket, extended it to full length, showed Annie Marie how to use it, and handed it to her. As he did, he remembered his first visit to the Hart estate, two years earlier, at the beginning of the 1878 shipping season. Hart's carriage driver had escorted Lane into a parlor as large and tall as Lane's boyhood home. The room had mahogany floor, walls, and ceiling, and six floor-to-ceiling windows which, when opened, became doors leading to outdoor gardens.

The parlor centerpiece was a stone fireplace big enough for a man to walk into without stooping. Above the fireplace hung a life-sized oil painting of a woman with pale, glowing skin, green eyes, and red hair. She was dressed in a high-collared burgundy dress and seated lightly on a stool, as if about to turn away from the viewer to face her spinet and raise her long, delicate fingers to the black and white keys.

A man's voice, deep and seasoned, had spoken from behind Lane: "My wife was beautiful, was she not, Mr. Lane?"

Lane had turned and for the first time faced the man who had summoned him. "Chief Mate Theodore Lane, at your service, sir."

"The consumption took her from me, five years ago."

"I'm sorry, sir."

"I have ten ships, Mr. Lane. Ten tall, fast, fine ships. But I'd load them all with gold and give them to God if He would give her back to me."

"Yes, sir."

Turning away from the painting of his wife, Hart had looked at Lane and said, "Please, tell about your sailing experience."

"Fine, sir," Lane had replied. "I grew up near the Milwaukee Harbor. Dad worked the harbor as a stevedore and took me aboard my first ship, the *Whiskey Pete*, when I was a small boy. As soon as I set foot on that ship, I knew I would become a sailor – and one day, a captain. When of age, I was hired by Captain Judson Wells as an Ordinary Seaman on his schooner, *North Star*. After one season, he made me Able-bodied Seaman. Two seasons ago, he made me his Chief Mate."

Hart had pulled a folded letter from his coat pocket and said, "Read this letter, Mr. Lane."

Lane had taken the letter, unfolded it, and read, aloud:

May 5, 1878
Dear Mr. Hart,
I trust that you are well. I am of sound mind and
body and getting the North Star *ready for my 35th*
sailing season. But let me come to my point. My Chief
Mate, Theodore Lane, is the finest Chief Mate I have ever
commanded. He has the instincts to be a captain – a way
with men, an understanding of sea and ship, a high
regard for all things maritime. I have held back nothing
from him, teaching him all that I know, giving him
command of my vessel whenever prudent. He will, one
day soon, become captain of his own ship.
In Highest Regards,
Judson Wells, Captain and Master
Schooner North Star

Astonished by the letter, Lane had said, "Captain Wells is generous."

"Judson Wells is an old friend," Hart had replied. "He is rarely so generous unless impressed by steady excellence. This letter is his way of telling me to hire you – before someone else does. Will you oblige me and join my fleet as Captain?"

A shiver of joy had run up and down Lane's spine. His lifelong desire to become a captain had led him to this moment, this place, this man, this offer. He had spoken without reservation: "I will indeed, sir. Which vessel?"

"The *Julia Hart*, the ship I named after my wife."

Annie Marie interrupted Lane's memory. "Oh — I see my father's home now!" she said, still looking through Lane's telescope. "The black shutters! The Observatory! Perhaps Father is in it now, watching us pass." She took the telescope away from her eye, raised her arm, and waved, as if she were able to see her father, and he, her. Turning to Lane, she set down the telescope, took his hands in her pale, delicate hands and asked, "Do you remember when we first met?"

"I do indeed," Lane said, smiling. "Your father led me up the stairs to the Observatory. And you were there, looking out over the lake."

Annie Marie offered the next detail. "Father said, 'Annie Marie, meet Captain Lane,' and I curtsied to you." Annie Marie smiled, lifted her skirt slightly and bent her knees, reenacting her first curtsey to him.

Lane chuckled and said, "Your father turned to me and said, 'Captain Lane, meet my daughter,' and I bowed to you." Lane bowed deeply, as he had at their first meeting.

Annie Marie giggled and asked, "Do you recall what happened next?"

"Every detail!" Lane said. "You looked me up and down and said, 'Captain Lane. Your eyes match the color of the lake.'"

"I was right! They do!" she said, looking again at his gray-blue eyes.

Lane laughed and said, "When you left us, your father said to me, 'I will do anything to see that she flourishes.'"

Annie Marie lost her smile and said, "He lost Mother. He cannot bear the thought of losing me." She took a deep breath of brisk air, smiled again, and said, "Here I am, sailing upon waters

I have only watched from afar!" She bent toward Lane, offered him her cheek, and received his kiss. The sails flapped twice, as if applauding, and the wind picked up to fifteen knots. The *Julia Hart*, on her last voyage of the 1880 season, was finally making good time.

At noon, Lane joined Annie Marie and her attendant for lunch in the Captain's Quarters. The three sat around the table, eating ham-and-bean porridge with spoons. Annie Marie asked Theodore many questions about the sea, the wind, and sailing. He, in turn, asked her many questions about their wedding ceremony, now just a fortnight away. After lunch, Annie Marie lay down on one bunk and took a long nap while her attendant sat on the other bunk, watching the cloudless sky through the small window above her bunk.

Near sunset, Torgeson came up to Lane and said, "Manitowoc Lighthouse at one point on the port bow." The *Julia Hart* sailed past Manitowoc, known as Clipper City because of the sailing ships built and launched from its shipyards, including, in 1874, the *Julia Hart*. Just as in Milwaukee, a row of tall, solid, brick estates stood along the lake north of downtown, built by friends and peers of David Lawrence Hart.

At dusk, Torgeson lit the running lanterns – red on port, green on starboard. One sailor climbed the foremast and lit the white lantern at the masthead, forty feet above the deck, while another sailor walked to the bow and stood lookout. Lane studied the Wisconsin shore, knowing that lighthouse keepers up and down the shore would be lighting their thousand-candle lanterns and beginning their night vigil for the sake of all those on the lake. Facing a night without much sleep, Lane momentarily envied them, thinking, at least they get to sleep during the day! His next thought cancelled out his envy: But they miss all this! Like most captains on the Great Lakes, he loved what he had: a ship sailing "full and by" beneath him, a sky above, a fine crew, and now, a beloved on board.

As soon as it got dark, Annie Marie asked her attendant to light the oil lamp strapped to the captain's desk, and as soon as the quarters filled with lamplight, Annie Marie walked to her spinet, sat on the stool, lifted the keyboard cover, and began to play. Warm yellow light and delicate music poured out through the curtained windows, and for a moment, every sailor aboard the *Julia Hart* paused and listened. Lane did not recognize the tune played by his beloved and thought, if I am to be a good husband to her, I must learn more about music!

The *Julia Hart* was two miles off Kewaunee when the wind shifted suddenly, as if God had turned a page in heaven and started another story on earth. Lane felt the wind-shift on his face and heard it ripple the sails above him. He checked the dark sky to the west and noticed that the stars, visible only minutes earlier, were hidden by clouds. But the Pole Star still shone brightly off the bow, as if leading them north, on course to Fish Creek, to their wedding and a new life as husband and wife.

Lane walked up to the young sailor at the wheel and ordered, "Hold course." He went below deck and checked the barometer. "Twenty-nine point eighty-four and falling," he said to himself, frowning. A falling barometer indicated worsening weather. He put on his wool coat and checked the barrels of salt stacked four high in the hold, wanting to be certain that the cargo was stowed securely.

Back on deck, Lane knocked on the door to the Captain's Quarters. Maggie Clark, the maidservant, opened the door a crack. "Yes?" she asked.

"Is Annie Marie well?" Lane inquired.

"She's seasick." Maggie studied Lane's face, illuminated by the lamplight behind her. "Is something wrong, Captain Lane?"

"We're securing for a blow," Lane answered, reluctantly. He entered and turned from her, closing and securing the wooden shutters over each window in the Captain's Quarters.

After dark, the southeast wind stiffened to twenty knots, and Lane saw the first spray coming off waves of ten feet. Lane made his rounds and told each crew member, "Barometer at twenty-nine point sixty-four and falling." Theodore pulled up his collar and looked up at the sails, each equipped with reef points, allowing a crew to shorten them. Lane found his Chief Mate and said, "Reef the sails."

Lane kept a sailor's eye on the sky as the wind and waves gained strength. The harvest moon broke out between two banks of clouds, a moon warm and cold at once, yellow in hue with silver and blue shadows. The ship, sailing at nearly fifteen knots, began to pitch and roll so that walking – even standing – became difficult. Lane judged the waves to be running between twelve and fifteen feet. He looked up at the masts and sails, their tops hidden by the night, and shouted, "Strike the mainsail!"

The wind kept stiffening, and the crew made more sail adjustments. The sheers, which held up the masts, were made of hemp and stretched and groaned with each wind gust, giving and taking, allowing the masts to sway like tree trunks in a storm. The wind, as if fed by the dark, built to forty knots, and the *Julia Hart* rose and fell on the waves, her bow cutting through them like a plough cutting through a rise in the soil.

Annie Marie, clutching a wash bowl, grew more seasick and wondered why her beloved was not with her, comforting her. "This is dreadful, Maggie," she said, weakly. "Had I imagined the voyage as it is now, I'd have done the sensible thing and traveled to Fish Creek by train." Her stomach rose into her throat, and she plunged her face into the bowl.

A knock on the door.

Maggie, on her knees next to Annie Marie, shouted, "Come in, please!"

Captain Lane opened the door and entered, seeing his beloved's distress. He took the wash bowl out of Annie Marie's hands, turned, tossed the vomit out the door onto the wet deck, and handed the empty bowl back to Maggie.

Annie Marie wiped her mouth with a handkerchief and said, "I am sick to death, Theodore. Can you stay with me?"

Realizing that she did not understand what was required of him as the captain of a vessel in a blow, Lane shook his head and said, "I must get back on deck, my love – but I will check on you again soon." He bent toward her, laid his palm across her forehead, turned and left. The desk lamp, low in oil, flickered and sparked.

Just after midnight, the lookout reported, "Sturgeon Bay Light at one point off the port bow!"

Lane made his way to Torgeson, eager to confer with his Chief Mate. Both men clutched sheers and stood unusually close in order to hear each other, the wind now strong enough to sweep words overboard. Lane pointed toward the Sturgeon Bay Lighthouse and Weather Bureau, and shouted above the wind, "How in God's name did Claflin predict this blow?"

Torgeson simply shook his head and shrugged his shoulders.

Lane shouted, "Winds out of the southeast. Waves at twenty feet. Barometer steady, so we must be running about even with the storm center."

"What say you, Captain?"

Thinking out loud, Lane said, "If we sought shelter now, we'd hang up on a reef, would we not?"

"It is likely, " shouted Torgeson.

Lane nodded, adding, "So we sail – like the Devil himself is after us!"

Wishing that he had only his ship, crew, and cargo to worry about, Lane grabbed a lantern, made his way across the deck, and checked on his passengers. Both women were lying face-down on their beds, clutching the mattresses beneath them. The quarters were pitch dark and stunk of vomit.

Lane filled the lamp with oil, the pitch and roll of the ship causing him to spill half a pint of acrid petroleum on the floor. He re-lit the wick and knelt next to his beloved's bunk, the bunk he himself used on most nights. She turned over and looked at him, a buffalo-hide blanket covering her body, her face as white as the spray off the waves. A wave crashed over the ship's stern, and a moment later, a drop of water dripped onto Lane's bare neck and rolled down his back, making him shiver.

"Have we sailed into hell?" asked Annie Marie.

"We are north of Sturgeon Bay and taking a beating. Stay in the cabin and you'll be fine." Lane again pressed his open hand against her warm forehead and added, "I had so wanted you to enjoy your first voyage."

She nodded, touched his hand, and closed her eyes.

The *Julia Hart* tried to outrun the Devil, but the Devil kept gaining on her, and the barometer kept falling. By the time the schooner sailed past the Baileys Harbor Light, the wind blew at fifty knots. Waves as high as twenty-five feet crashed against her stern, sprayed her deck, and lifted her three-hundred tons as if she were an empty salt barrel floating on the water.

Lane, aware that his bid to outrun the storm center had failed, aware that he was in the midst of a blow worse than any he'd ever experienced, needed a new strategy. He could think of only two choices: Heave to, which would mean shortening the sails, coming about, and facing the ship directly into the storm – or searching the dark reef-lined shore for shelter. Neither choice heartened him.

Captain Lane again spoke with his Chief Mate, shouting, "Have you ever been in such a blow?"

Torgeson shook his head. "My father told stories about a blow like this in the Baltic, off Sweden. Fifty ships and four hundred sailors lost at sea." Lane was about to order a heave-to and face into the wind, but Torgeson pointed ahead and shouted, "The Cana Island Light!"

Lane turned, nodded, and shouted, "Her lee is fine shelter with a bold shore, is it not?"

"Yes – and her Light would give us a bearing."

Lane, enormously relieved, leaned into Torgeson, and said, "To the lee of Cana Island!"

Torgeson communicated Lane's order to the sailor at the wheel, and Lane made his way to Annie Marie's quarters. He knocked on the door and entered. The spinet, upended by the toss of a wave, lay on its face at his feet, the black and white keys crushed against the deck. Annie Marie stared at the ceiling, eyes wide with terror, refusing to acknowledge her beloved's presence in any way, as if her spirit had left her body. Maggie Clark knelt alongside Annie Marie's bunk, her head against Annie Marie's hip.

"Can you hear me, Annie Marie?" Lane shouted.

Annie Marie did not move or speak, but Maggie lifted her head.

"We are nearing shelter, Miss Clark," Lane said. "Take heart."

The Cana Island Light was a white brick tower with a lantern set at one hundred feet above the lake. Waves rolled across the island's beach and crashed against the lighthouse door. The Light house Keeper, William Sanderson, watched a wave sweep away his flock of caged chickens. He hurried down the lighthouse stairs, waded through ankle-deep water to his house, and escorted his wife and three children into the lighthouse tower, closing the tower door behind them just as a wave crashed against it. "Up the stairs!" he yelled. "The whole island is going under!"

The *Julia Hart* stood off Cana Island on a port tack, and Lane and his Chief Mate got their first look at the island lee.

"Stacked up!" Torgeson shouted, alarmed. Three ships — lanterns glowing, sails down — were already anchored in the island's lee, their dark shapes rising and falling on the waves.

"Come about!" ordered Lane.

Annie Marie felt the *Julia Hart* swing hard to port, and she rose to her elbows in bed. With its forward momentum, the vessel drew close to the lee of the island, a hundred yards from the port side of an anchored scow. Torgeson hung over the bow, swung a lead into the water, and called out the depth to Lane, who stood right behind him. At five fathoms, Lane turned to two sailors and shouted, "Let go the starboard anchor four shots on deck."

The anchor chain rattled and dragged against the deck, and the anchor plunged into the water, digging into the sand, halting the *Julia Hart* in thirty feet of water, a hundred yards from the lee shore of Cana Island.

Hearing the anchor drop, Maggie Clark got on her feet. She opened the door and stepped out into the wind just as a wave came across the starboard stern, slammed the door shut behind her, took her feet out from under her, and swept her over the port deck railing into the lake, into the night.

Several minutes later, an unexpected and violent concussion shook Annie Marie out of her stupor. Terrified, she raised her head and looked for her attendant, but saw only an empty bunk. Annie Marie got up and stumbled to the door, wondering, where is Maggie? As soon as Annie Marie got on deck, the wind filled her long skirt like a sail and carried her against – and almost over – the port deck railing.

Lane, near midship, saw Annie Marie and hurried to her across the slick deck, but just before he reached her, the ship suffered another violent concussion, and he fell backwards, banging his head against the deck. Dizzy, he sat up, shook his head, and watched Annie Marie come to him on her hands and knees, her clothes and hair soaked by the time she reached him. She helped Lane to his feet just as another violent concussion shook the vessel. "What is happening?" Annie Marie shouted.

"We're pounding bottom!" Lane answered.

Torgeson came to them with bad news. "The anchor is

dragging!"

Lane shook his head, trying to regain his senses, and shouted, "Slack the anchor to five shots."

Lane turned to Annie Marie and said, "It's not safe on deck. Get back to your quarters."

"Where is Maggie?" she shouted.

Torgeson ran up again, shaking his head. "It's no good. We're still dragging anchor."

Lane glanced at the island's shore, the lighthouse, and at the other ships. "God damn it!" he shouted. "The other ships are holding, why can't we?"

"Perhaps they're lighter, sir."

The shore fell away beneath the *Julia Hart*, dropping beyond the reach of the anchor, allowing the ship to drift freely, stern first.

"Hoist the anchor and raise sail!" Lane ordered.

Torgeson nodded and ran off, and Lane took Annie Marie's hand and escorted her back to the Captain's Quarters. He stood with her in the open doorway, putting his arms around her, keeping his eyes on the dark ahead of their rapid drift.

"Can you see anything?" Lane asked.

"What are we looking for?" she answered.

Lane did not reply. He turned around and watched his crew open the storm sail, which rippled like rifle shots and ballooned with wind. With Annie Marie still in his arms, he leaned so that he could see around the quarters and noticed that the lighthouse beacon – now a half-mile away from his vessel – was at one point on the starboard bow. This meant that his ship, as if given an order to come about, was beginning a turn that would put its bow in the lead. This heartened Lane.

As the ship turned broadside to the wind and waves, Annie Marie shouted, "Trees!"

Lane turned and shuddered when he made out the treeline, blacker than the thick sky, off the port side. Instantly, he knew that his ship was going to be blown into the fast-approaching peninsula shore and that no order could change that fate. He turned to Annie Marie and shouted, "Brace yourself!"

The keel hit rock and brought the *Julia Hart* to a sudden halt, driving Lane and Marie against – and almost over – the port railing, toppling a few salt barrels in the hold. The bow of the ship swung toward shore, lifted by waves and blown by winds until the three-masted schooner grounded broadside against a shore so bold that the trees were only thirty feet off the vessel's port side.

A wave crashed against the *Julia Hart* like a battering ram, lifting and tilting her toward shore, sending water and spray up and over Annie Marie and Lane. A second wave hit the ship, and a third, each wave shifting the cargo and tilting the ship. Lane pushed Annie Marie back into the Captain's Quarters just as Torgeson came up to him. "Search the vessel for Annie Marie's attendant and then assemble the crew here!" Lane shouted.

Lane stood in the open doorway of his quarters and looked out, up, and around, surveying every detail of their desperate situation. One by one, his crew of eight made their way across the drenched, sloping deck and into the Captain's Quarters, nodding to Lane as they passed him in the doorway and crowding onto the empty bunk across from Annie Marie. A wave hit the vessel and sent a few more barrels of salt tumbling below deck. Lane asked solemnly, "Did anyone find Miss Clark?"

Torgeson said, "She's no longer on board, Captain."

"Oh God!" cried Annie Marie.

Lane sat on the bunk next to his beloved, put his arm around her, looked at his crew, and declared, "This vessel is no longer safe. On my word, we will abandon ship."

"Shall we unlash the yawl?" asked Torgeson.

"What yawl?" Lane answered.

All heads turned to the doorway and all eyes looked toward the stern, where they expected to see a small wooden boat lashed to the railing. But the boat was gone, torn from its lashing, swept into the woods and broken in two around the trunk of a white pine.

Torgeson looked at Lane and asked, "Do we swim to shore?"

"No. We climb."

Puzzled, Torgeson asked, "Climb?"

"The shore is bold and our tilt is severe, so the mizzen is caught in the trees. We climb up the mizzen and climb down a tree."

Another wave struck and lifted the vessel, and the toppled barrels of salt rolled back and forth beneath the Captain's Quarters. Sailors were skilled at climbing, but in such a blow, and with waves pounding against the grounded ship, climbing a mast or rope ladder or ratline would be no ordinary undertaking.

Lane turned to his Chief Mate and said, "You first, Soren. If you make it, we'll all follow, one by one."

Torgeson nodded, stood, laid his hand on Lane's shoulder, and left. Lane, Annie Marie, and the crew gathered just outside the Captain's Quarters and watched Torgeson make his way to the mizzen.

He was halfway up the mizzen's rope ladder when the first

wave hit, jolting the ship, nearly jerking him off the ladder. He held on, climbed higher, and grabbed hold of the standing rigging just as another wave lifted and rocked the ship. Torgeson lost his footing and hung by his hands from the rigging. For a few moments his feet flailed the air high above the churning water between the ship and shore. Then the Swede regained his footing and grabbed the branches of a tree tangled with the mizzen.

"He made it!" Lane shouted, relieved.

One by one, the crew, inspired by Torgeson's success, climbed the mast and got to shore, until only Lane and Annie Marie remained on the *Julia Hart*. A wave hit the ship, and foam rushed across the deck like whitewater over a river rapids. Lane pulled Annie Marie back into the Captain's Quarters, now awash in ankle-deep, frigid water.

Annie Marie, her voice trembling with fear and cold, said, "I can't do what those men did."

"You can and you must!"

This was too much for her, and her eyes closed, her head fell to her chest, and her knees buckled.

"Annie Marie!" Lane caught her as she slumped and held her limp body against him. He bent over, let her body fall across his shoulder, and stood, his arm around her waist, her arms hanging down his back and her legs across his chest. Now he had to do what Torgeson and the other men did, but he had to do it while carrying his beloved.

Lane hurried to the mizzen. Using all his strength and balance, he began to climb the rope ladder with Annie Marie across his shoulder. He climbed slowly, pulling upward with his hands, pushing upward with his feet, resting each time he gained a rung. He made steady progress until a wave hit the ship, nearly knocking him and Annie Marie into the churning, dark water below. Awakened and disoriented by the jolt, Annie Marie began to struggle against Lane's grip and pound his back with her fists. He ignored her protests and continued his climb.

The tree branches were nearly within Lane's reach when the next wave hit the vessel, and he had to throw both arms around the mizzen in order to avoid falling, pinning Annie Marie's writhing body between him and the mast. Exhausted and winded, Lane doubted that he had enough strength left to get them both to safety.

"Captain!"

Startled, Lane looked up and saw Torgeson, who had, unnoticed by Lane, climbed back up the tree, crossed to the mast, and was now just above Lane and offering his hand. Lane tried to calm Annie Marie so that he could lift her to Torgeson, but Annie Marie, beside herself with terror, could not be quieted or stilled.

Seeing that Annie Marie's struggles endangered both herself and his captain, Torgeson made a boxer's fist, leaned down, and struck Annie Marie across the cheek. Her head jerked at the force of his blow, then dropped against her chest. Torgeson hefted Annie Marie's limp body onto his shoulder, turned, and grabbed a sturdy tree branch.

Lane looked at Annie Marie seated next to him in the carriage, asleep, a black pillow between her swollen, cut cheek and the carriage wall. A wool blanket covered her legs. Though eight o'clock in the morning, it was still dark as night, the sun obscured by thick, black clouds. Rain pelted the carriage windows, and the wind, now gusting to ninety miles an hour, rocked the rolling carriage and whistled through cracks and openings in the carriage cab. Broken tree limbs and fallen trees lay across the muddy road, forcing the driver to slow his horses and maneuver his carriage over or around the storm litter.

Lane had given the driver twenty dollars in gold to travel in such weather across the Door County Peninsula to Fish Creek, where Lane figured that Annie Marie's father now waited, uncertain of his daughter's fate, blind with fear. Lane looked at Annie Marie and lifted his hand to touch her, but not wanting to wake her, halted his hand just shy of her cheek.

Near noon, the carriage driver reined his winded, mud-splattered horses to a stop in front of the Fish Creek Captain's Club. A dozen men came out of the Club's front door and rushed to the carriage. Annie Marie, still weak, emerged from the carriage but was blown back in it by a gust of wind. Lane and several other men got her out of the carriage and walked her into the Club's front parlor.

"Annie Marie!" Mr. Hart broke through the crowd surrounding his daughter and took her in his arms. "Oh, thank God! Thank God!" He buried his face in her matted hair. She began to cry, softly, happy to be back in her father's arms which had protected her so well all her life.

Hart looked up at Lane and said, "Thank you for returning my daughter to me safely, Captain Lane."

Lane nodded.

"What happened?" Hart asked.

"The blow hit us at night off Kewaunee. We tried to outrun her —"

"You tried to outrun her?" Hart interrupted, incredulous. "With my daughter aboard, you tried to outrun such a storm rather than seek shelter?" Hart pressed Annie Marie's head tight against his chest.

"We did not know we were up against such a fierce blow until it was well upon us, and then we sought shelter in the lee made by Cana Island, north of –"

"I know where Cana Island is, Captain!" Hart's lips began to tremble. "But I don't know where my ship is!"

"We dragged anchor and drifted onto a bold shore north of the island."

"The *Julia Hart* is stranded?"

"Yes."

"Where is Miss Clark?"

Lane looked down and said, quietly, "Swept overboard."

Hart winced, as if stuck with a knife, silent. Fearing the worst, he asked, "Where is your crew?"

"My crew has taken refuge in the home of a fisherman. They await my return."

Hart looked down at his daughter, put a single finger under her chin, and gently lifted her head so that he could see her face. He frowned when he noticed the cut and bruise on her cheek.

Annie Marie, as if she were a young girl telling her father about a bad dream, blurted out, "Maggie just disappeared, and the rest of us had to climb the mast and jump into the trees!"

Hart glared at Lane and asked, "Is this so, Captain?"

"It is, sir. We –"

"Captain Lane!" Hart interrupted. "My daughter will never again board your vessel."

"Yes, sir," Lane said, looking down.

"Nor will she marry you."

Startled, Captain Lane looked up at his employer.

Hart added, "Do I make myself clear?"

"Sir ... you cannot do this."

"I have done it, Captain," Hart said, his lips twitching with fury.

Lane knew that the next move belonged to Annie Marie, so he watched her and waited, expecting her to protest her father's startling command. But instead, she remained silent and buried her head deeper into her father's chest.

Stunned, Lane stared at Annie Marie. After a moment, he looked at the faces of the people in the parlor, all strangers. A gust of wind blew through the open door, fluttering curtains, lifting papers off the parlor table, and blowing the shock and confusion out of his mind like fog out of a harbor. Lane thought, I do not want to marry a woman whose love for me is not as strong as the wind at sea. God has saved us both from making a terrible blunder!

"I can also relieve you of your command, Captain." Hart said, with menace.

Calm for the first time since the blow began, Lane looked at his employer and said, "You can, sir, but you will not."

"And why is that, Captain?"

"I am no loss to you as a son-in-law, sir. But I am a great loss to you as a captain."

Hart's trembling lips stretched into an odd smile, a smile as taut as a ship's rigging in a blow. "Is the *Julia Hart* salvageable, Captain?"

"She will sail again, sir."

"Return to your ship, Captain."

"Right away, sir." Lane looked once more at the back of Annie Marie's head, turned away from her – and the life he thought he would have with her – and walked back to the carriage, eager to return to his crew and right his vessel.

SHOW YOUR WORK

Jim's NOTE, FOLDED INTO AN AIRPLANE, glided onto my open geometry book. The note read: "What'd you do all summer?"

Beneath his question, I wrote, "Burned bodies!"

Mr. Knauer, coming from behind me, pinned the open note to my desk with the rubber tip of his hardwood pointer. He took the note, read it, arched his bushy blond right eyebrow, and looked down at me. "Hank," he said. "I'm waiting for an explanation."

"I worked at Eternal Flame Memorial Park."

"And you burned bodies there?" he asked.

"Yes – in the crematorium."

Always interested in numbers, Knauer asked, "How many bodies?"

"On a good day I could burn four." The guys made faces. The girls – with the exception of Karen – groaned. They're all jealous, I thought, knowing that they had spent their summers flipping hamburgers, sweeping floors, and stacking boxes. The bell rang and got me off the hook.

Jim walked beside me down the hall, and we stopped at my locker. "How do you do it?" he asked.

"Do what?"

"Burn bodies."

I opened my locker and told him the secret recipe: "We slide them in a big cooker – casket and all – and bake them at twenty-six hundred degrees for three hours." I dropped my geometry book onto the bottom of my locker and slammed the metal door shut. Jim jumped. "You know what's left after baking?"

"What?" Jim asked, eyes wide.

"Hip sockets. Skull chunks."

"Jesus!"

"We shovel the sockets and chunks into the crusher, which grinds them to ashes, and we put the ashes into an urn and say, 'Here's your husband, Ma'am.'"

The next day, Jim and Karen stood at Knauer's classroom door, eyeing me, which made me nervous. I liked Karen but never knew what to say to her. In sixth grade, I had sat behind her, often staring at her shiny hair falling down her back like a blonde waterfall – and staring, between her blouse and backbone, at her bra, and the lovely little clasp which undid the whole thing.

Smiling, Karen said to me, "We want to see that oven."

I wanted to say, "I could lose my job." Instead, I said, "Okay."

"Great!" she said. "When?"

"Let me figure that out."

"Can I bring Bill?" she asked.

My heart sank. Bill was her boyfriend, a crewcut jock with arms like logs and legs like tree trunks, a Varsity running back who had won last year's homecoming game by dragging three tacklers with him across the goal line.

"Bring him," I said, unable to say no to her.

In geometry class, I was trying to solve my problem: How can I show her the oven without getting fired?

"Hank!" Knauer shouted, making me jump and look up. He held the tip of his pointer against an isosceles triangle drawn on the blackboard in white chalk. "What's the next step to this problem?" he asked.

"I was working out another problem, Mr. Knauer."

"I see. Would you like to put that problem on the board?"

"No … it's too complicated."

Karen turned around and smiled at me.

Knauer frowned and said, "Detention. After school, today."

At three o'clock, I walked into Knauer's classroom and sat at my desk. Knauer was washing the front blackboard, his back to me. Without turning around, he said, "Do the problems on page nineteen and show your work." He sat at his desk and began grading papers, the bald spot at the top of his head pointing my way, an evil eye. Turning my attention to the first problem, I got to work.

By Friday, I had solved my more complicated problem.

After geometry class, I said to Karen, "Meet me at the front gate of the cemetery tomorrow night, eight sharp – behind the big bushes."

"Terrific! I'll tell Jim and Bill," she said.

I got to the cemetery gate just before eight, leaned against the ten-foot-tall iron-spike fence which surrounded the graveyard, and listened to the stiff warm breeze blow through the junipers. The sound calmed me and made me forget the yelling match between Mom and Dad at dinner.

Karen, Jim, and Bill showed up at eight sharp, but they were not alone. Bill carried a naked, life-sized, plastic man-without-genitals under his arm. "What's that?" I asked, surprised.

Bill set the beige man on his feet in front of me, and Karen said, "A mannequin. My dad owns a clothes store, and we got a dozen of these in our garage. Let's call him, 'Mr. Knauer.'"

"Why did you bring him?" I asked.

"So we could put him in the oven and watch him burn."

I liked her idea.

At five after eight, Eddy, the night watchman, a skinny man of sixty who smoked fat cigars, drove past us and turned onto Capitol Drive. "He's on dinner break," I said. "We got an hour. Let's go."

We ran, single-file and bent low, toward the mausoleum. It wasn't completely dark, but the four-story stone building was already lit up by the night spotlights like a castle. I got out my key, opened the back door, and said, "Get in." The metal door boomed shut behind us, and we stood in the dark.

Bill whispered, "Turn on the lights."

"No lights. No loud noises," I said. "If Eddy comes back early, I don't want him to see or hear us." I pulled my olive-green Boy Scout flashlight out of my back pocket, turned it on, and said, "Follow me."

We left the entryway and walked down a long hall, the sound of our footsteps echoing against the marble floor and walls in such a way that it seemed like we'd been joined by a dozen invisible people. Using the light beam as a pointer, I said, "Those are crypts – eight high. We pull off the marble front plate, roll in a casket, and seal that baby up air-tight. My boss says that the bodies in here don't rot, they just dry up and become mummies."

"This place gives me the creeps," Bill said.

"Here's the elevator," I said. "Get in." I pulled the iron gate shut behind us and pushed the B button. The elevator jerked and whined, lowering us – and the mannequin – into the basement. Proud of my unusual work, I narrated our journey: "We take the caskets downstairs in this elevator."

Jim sniffed loudly. "Smells funny in here."

Karen looked at me and asked, "What happens to people after they die?"

"I don't know," I said. "But people have souls – that much I know from working here."

"Have you seen somebody's soul?" Bill asked, his voice blending alarm and doubt.

"No. But I've felt .. a presence."

"Shut up!" Jim said.

Bill made the sign of the cross over his chest.

"Why do you work in a place like this?" Karen asked me.

"At home, there's lots of yelling and fighting. Here, it's peaceful and quiet."

The elevator jerked to a stop. I pulled back the gate and said, "To your left, folks, the crematorium is to your left." Bill was at home between the goal posts, but now he was on my turf.

We walked into a vast room with concrete walls and twenty-foot ceilings crisscrossed with pipes big enough to crawl through. Pointing with my flashlight, I explained, "That's the cooker. That's the crusher." As we passed a casket, I ran my hand along the smooth enameled cover and said, "Standard metal casket. Empty."

"You sure it's empty?" asked Jim.

Running my hand to the cover's edge, I lifted it suddenly and shined the light beam into the padded, upholstered interior.

"Don't ever do that again," Bill said, his voice thin.

I left the casket lid open.

When we got to the oven, I gave Karen my flashlight and spun the steel wheel, which raised the heavy oven door. "Here goes," I said, pushing the start-up button.

The oven rumbled and moaned like an old man waking up. A red glow appeared at the back of the oven, and its light poured toward us like a living presence. Bill set the mannequin on its feet and took a step back.

"Hank – say a prayer for Knauer," Karen said, playfully.

"O Lord," I said. "Here is your earthly servant, Alfred Knauer. We are going to warm him up a bit, teach him how hot the flames of hell will be if he doesn't change his evil ways." Karen snickered, and she and I picked him up and slid him feet-first into the oven.

Bill grabbed my arm and yelled, "Wait!" His voice echoed off the concrete walls: *Wait! ... Wait! ... Wait!*

"Keep it down." I said.

Karen asked him, "What's your problem?"

He let go of my arm, looked at Karen, and said, "This could bring us bad luck." Ignoring his protest, Karen and I slid Knauer into the oven on his bare backside and stepped back. His skin began melting right away, like a slice of cheese on top of a hot hamburger. The burning plastic smelled a lot like the bodies I burned all summer.

Then a noise started coming from Knauer himself ... *Hsssssssssss!* ... like he was letting out his last breath of air. We all took a step back.

"What was that sound?" asked Jim, stepping back farther.

"That's the sound a dying man makes," Bill said, alarmed.

The noise coming from Knauer alarmed me too, but I thought: That must be the air seeping out of his hollow body cavity.

At that moment, Knauer's whole chest caved in and his arms came up slowly – like he was reaching over his head to grab us.

Bill and Jim backed away from the oven and bumped right into the open casket. The casket lid banged shut. Bill leapt forward, took me by the shoulders and shouted, "How do we get out of here?"

Out of here! ... Out of here! ... Out of here!

His eyes darted wildly, searching for a way out. I shined the light beam on the back stairway, and he and Jim took those concrete steps three at a time. Bill hit the steel exit door like he hit those two-hundred-pound tacklers: *Boom!*

Boom! ... Boom! ... Boom!

The door clicked shut behind them. Alone with Karen for the first time since sixth grade, I looked right at her and she looked right at me and boy was she fine, and we burst out laughing, laughing like hell and death was nothing as Knauer melted his way from this world to the next.

A FURIOUS WILT

Most rose bushes don't live past twenty, but that *Mister Lincoln* which Ethel planted in memory of her husband lived past thirty and put out blood-red blossoms larger than her open hand. Each time she showed that *Mister Lincoln* to someone, she said, "If you take care of something, it will last a long time."

Ethel planted her second rose bush, a *Viking Queen*, in memory of her daughter Sarah, her only child, who was killed in a car wreck three years after she lost Emil. She described the color of Sarah's *Viking Queen* as "that pink in the sky before the sun comes up."

Over the years, Ethel had planted a rose bush in memory of each person she had known and lost, and now, at seventy, she has dozens of rose bushes divided into four round raised beds. Last spring, Ethel's neighbor, Mr. Langendorf, had asked her if she would like help tending her rose beds, but she would not have it. Ethel did all the work herself: sprayed, dusted, fertilized, pruned, winterized, all without gloves. "If I was afraid of a few scratches," she once said, "I'd raise petunias."

In June, Ethel's parish, St. Peter and Paul, received a new priest,

Father John Nauth, and during a luncheon address to the Confraternity of the Holy Rosary, he introduced himself by saying, "I consider myself a traditional man – I love wine, women, and roses." The women stirred and murmured, and Father John paused, enjoying the commotion.

"But since I am a priest," he added, "I focus my love on the wine of the Sacrament, the woman of our Blessed Virgin, and ... well ... with roses, I love them all, without restraint!" Relieved, the women laughed and Father John smiled.

After his address, two of Ethel's Holy Rosary friends, Phyllis Rinder and Lucy Mahlberg, scurried up to Father John. Phyllis said, "Father – if you love roses, you'll want to go by Ethel Klesen's at 525 Sixth Street. It's the little white house with royal-blue shutters and round rose beds." Though Ethel's friends did not tell Father Nauth, they also thought that a visit from him might encourage Ethel to return to her parish which, at one time, she had visited every morning for Mass.

The next morning, Ethel looked out of her front window and saw a tall, slender, silver-haired stranger standing on the sidewalk in front of her home, admiring her sidewalk rose bed. He was dressed in black from neck to toe, except for a patch of white across his throat. She opened her royal-blue front door and looked at the priest without speaking. Father John looked up and introduced himself, adding, "I just planted a few roses myself, in the rectory garden. But they're not so ..." He paused, searching for the right word. He loved and knew many words, in English, Latin, German, Greek, and Spanish. "... handsome. Yes, that's the word, they're not so handsome as yours."

This compliment drew Ethel through the door and onto the

front porch.

"What's your secret?" he asked.

"Love," she said.

He nodded.

"And cow manure," she added.

Father John laughed, which coaxed Ethel down her front steps. He pointed to a rose blossom in her sidewalk bed and asked, "That rose with deep purple petals and lavender stripes – what's its name?"

"*Purple Tiger*," she said. "The only tiger in town."

"And ready to roar!" Father John said.

A moment later, she stood beside Father John on the sidewalk, pointing to and naming the other roses in her sidewalk bed: "*Iceberg. Peace. Solitude. Opening Night. Eternity ...*"

The priest got down on one knee and pressed his nose and cheeks into the face of a white blossom with delicate yellow washes at the edge of each pedal.

"*Victorian Lace*," Ethel said.

He closed his eyes, and took a deep, slow breath through his nostrils. "Mmmmmm ... such fragrance. Sweet, but also a touch ... fruity."

The two rose-lovers chatted for twenty minutes, and then Father John said, "I must be going, Mrs. Klesen, but what a pleasure to meet you and your roses. I am inspired!"

The next morning, Ethel woke up with Father John on her mind. She got up, dressed, and sat at her formica kitchen table, drinking a cup of Sanka, wondering what sort of gift she might give to the priest as a welcome to Kiel. Later that morning, she sank her spade into the pile of ripe cow manure behind her garage, filled a burlap bag with manure, and tied it shut with a red

Christmas ribbon. To the ribbon, she attached a note which read: "Father John. A gift for your roses. Ethel Klesen. *p.s.* Please call me Ethel from now on." She visited her neighbor and asked, "Mr. Langendorf, would you make a delivery for me today?"

Father John liked Ethel's gift so much that he phoned her and said, "Ethel. In gratitude for your unexpected gift, I am titling Sunday's homily, '*Scheisse!*' – the German word for manure."

Ethel's cheeks twitched when she heard him use that word, and after a moment, she said, "Yes, Father, I know the word. I must warn you, 'Scheisse!' may mean manure where you come from, but here it means ... well ... 'Scheisse!' is what we holler when we miss the nail with the hammer and hit our thumb."

Father John chuckled and said, "Such a title should create wide interest in my homily, don't you think?" The homily title, printed on the parish sign, did create interest, slowing cars and pedestrians on Main Street all week.

Phyllis phoned Ethel and said, "This is one homily you shouldn't miss."

Ethel did not attend Mass that Sunday, but the faithful and the curious packed the pews. In his homily, Father John told the story of Ethel's gift of manure. He concluded by saying, "Gift-giving is what God is all about. And when we give gifts to one another ... without strings attached, then we are in God's ..." He paused for a long time, searching for the right word. "... likeness. Yes, then we are in God's likeness."

Phyllis phoned Ethel from the parish office phone after Mass and said, "The crowd was bigger than Easter Sunday. I counted six Methodists, eight Lutherans, and ... I swear on the breast of our dear Virgin ... a Baptist – Mr. John Turnbrenner, the manager at Citizens Bank, who came without his wife and children, probably worried that it wasn't a homily for the whole family."

The day after Father John's "Scheisse!" homily, things heated up in Kiel. Phyllis phoned Ethel early on Monday morning and said, "It's ninety on my thermometer already. I bet we hit a hundred today."

On Tuesday, Emil's *Mister Lincoln* collapsed in a furious wilt, the tall green canes falling limp against the gnarled wood trunk. Ethel stood alongside the rose, soaking it with the hose but unable to bring it back. She thought, just like Emil. He could take the cold, but the heat finally got him.

That night, a full moon flooded Ethel's bedroom with a brilliant blue light. Whenever she closed her eyes, she saw Emil's body sprawled across the kitchen linoleum, face down, his fingers twitching, and finally, still. She comforted herself by thinking, we had twenty-eight years together. And I musn't forget that his *Mister Lincoln* lived ten years longer than I had any right to expect. She did a little calculation in her mind and concluded: That bush put out a good three thousand blossoms in his memory.

The next morning, Ethel found the *Sexy Rexy* that she had planted in memory of her lively sister, Elsie, limp as a fresh corpse, its fierce pink blossoms hanging face down in the dirt, as if ashamed. She soaked the bush for two hours, but it did not rebound.

Puzzled, Ethel put on her glasses, dropped to her knees in the soggy lawn and searched the bush for mites, scales, mildew, rust, cankers, aphids, and slugs. Nothing. She stood, put her fists on her hips, and glanced up at the relentless sun. A cicada buzzed from the branches of her backyard elm.

That evening, she sat on the porch swing until well past dark, still, except for her eyes, which searched her yard for invaders.

On Sunday, Ethel got up an hour earlier than usual and toured her rose beds even before she had her cup of Sanka. "Oh, no!" she said, coming upon Sarah's wilted *Viking Queen*. At that moment, the steeple bells at St. Peter and Paul began to bong and clatter. When she was a girl, those same bells had rung and her mother would say, "Hurry now, children! We'll be late for Mass!" Ethel had never minded Mass, but she had always hated confession, hated standing in line with the fat old women, hated stepping into the confessional which smelled like perfume and rouge and reminded her of a dark closet, hated the raspy voice of that "nosy old man with the collar," hated his unspoken demand that she share her lovely little secrets with him.

After she had married, Ethel quit confession, but she made Emil go each week, and when their daughter Sarah was old enough, she made Emil take her with him. Once, Emil had said to Ethel, "It don't seem right that we go without you. People think we're the only ones in this family with sins to confess." Ethel had replied, "I make my confession during Mass. That's my way and that's all there is to it" – which let Emil know that he had come up against something in her which "was, and is, and always will be. Amen."

After the car wreck, Sarah had clung to life for three days, and Ethel had stayed by her hospital bed in Sheboygan day and night, praying, "If a life must be taken, Lord, let it be mine."

The Lord did not accept her bargain.

Phyllis and Lucy had stood on each side of Ethel, holding her up, while she watched the pallbearers lower Sarah's metal casket into the stony earth, just seven days before Sarah's twenty-first birthday. At the priest's nod, Ethel had stooped down, picked up a handful of dirt and stones, stretched out her arm above Sarah's coffin, and opened her hand. The dirt and stones had fallen as a clump and banged against the coffin lid, a sound so harsh and forlorn that her eyes closed, her head dropped to her chest, and her knees wobbled and gave out. Later, Phyllis had said to the priest, "Ethel wilted in our hands like a cut rose, from top to bottom."

After Sarah's funeral, Ethel had begun to avoid Sunday Mass. Alarmed, Phyllis and Lucy had used both love and guilt to get her to back to Mass, but she had told them, "Why? What good has it ever done me?"

Helpless to know how to assist Sarah's fallen *Viking Queen*, Ethel resumed her tour of her rose beds, alert for trouble. She cut a creamy white blossom from a *Prince of Peace*, raised the rose to her chin, bent her head to meet the blossom, and inhaled slowly, drawing the fragrance into her nostrils and lungs. She placed the *Prince of Peace* blossom in a vase next to her painted plaster statue of the Virgin Mary. "Haven't I been through enough?" she said to the statue, in a voice which perfectly blended politeness and despair.

That Monday, Ethel lost two roses. On Tuesday, three. On Wednesday, five. She could not stop – or even explain – their deaths. On Friday, Mr. Langendorf stopped by to tell her that three of her bushes in the bed near their lot line had wilted and fallen. She pressed her lips together so tightly that they lost their color.

After her neighbor left, Ethel walked into her bedroom and

opened her slip drawer. She lifted the statue of Mary off her dresser and gently laid it face down on top of her folded white slips, and closed the drawer. The *Prince of Peace* blossom, now alone on the dresser, opened, wilted, browned, and fell to pieces, petal by petal.

The next morning, Father John walked by Ethel's house, expecting to see her in the yard or on the porch swing, but she was nowhere in sight. Her front door was open, so he turned onto her walkway. Peering through her screen door, he saw Ethel sitting on her front-room couch, hands in her lap, staring into her empty fireplace. He knocked on the screen door and asked, "Ethel, are you okay?"

She jerked her head toward him and said, "Father! I must show you what has happened to me." Ethel led Father John into the yard and showed him each wilted rose bush. She ended her tour at Sarah's *Viking Queen*.

"How can this be?" she asked.

Father John got down on one knee and lifted a wilted cane. He asked, "Did you check the roots?"

"Well, no."

"Bring me your spade!" He sunk her spade into the soft soil and unearthed the bush. They both expected to see a stiff tangle of roots but the roots were gone – cut off cleanly, as if by a knife. Astonished, Ethel shook her head.

The priest looked closely at the root stubs, stood, and held the bush in front of Ethel. "Teeth marks," he said. "Gophers." He looked around her yard and added, "They probably have tunnels all through your beds."

Ethel knew that the farmers' fields outside of town were full of gophers, but she had never seen a gopher in her yard or in town.

The thought of this underground invasion wilted Ethel's legs, and she collapsed to her knees in the thick grass. Father John threw the bush aside and helped her back onto her feet, across the yard, and onto the porch swing. He sat with her until she felt stronger. Ethel knew how to protect her roses against most pests, but she did not know how to defend her roses against gophers.

"Do you know how to get rid of gophers?" she asked Father John.

"No. But I'll ask around."

"I don't pray anymore, Father," she said, her voice trembling, dark, and hollow. Father John looked at her a long time, then sat back in his chair, closed his eyes, and nodded, saying nothing, but allowing her loneliness to meet his in the perfect quiet of that morning.

After Father John left, Ethel got Emil's old .22 rifle from the attic, locked a .22-short in the chamber, and sat on the porch swing with the rifle across her knees. Her farsightedness put her rose beds in perfect focus. Mr. Langendorf, repairing a chrome toaster in his garage workshop, flinched at the sharp report of Emil's rifle. He looked out his workshop window and saw Ethel hurrying to one of her rose beds, the rifle in the crook of her arm. He walked up to her and spoke in a voice raised with alarm, "Ethel Klesen, what's gotten into you? You can't shoot off a gun in town limits!"

Shame flooded her when she realized her recklessness. "I'm terribly sorry. I'll put this gun away right now."

That night, Ethel could not sleep. She checked the lighted electric clock face by her bed often and watched the brass second hand go round and round. As the night deepened, all her griefs came back to her, as if God had opened his hand above her and her griefs had fallen from his hand onto her chest, pressing down on her until she could take only shallow breaths.

At three o'clock, she got out of bed without turning on the light, opened the dresser drawer, and brought the statue of Mary back to her bed. Holding the statue against her chest, she examined the shape with her fingers, feeling the sweep of Mary's outstretched arms, the bow of her head, the delicate fingers of each open hand. Ethel's breathing relaxed and deepened, as if Mary's hands were lifting the griefs, one by one, off her chest.

The next morning, Father John knocked on Ethel's door. She opened the door and said, "Come in, Father. I have something to ask you."

They sat in her front room. Ethel, preparing a little speech in her mind, did not notice the paper sack in the priest's hand. "Father, last night, I …" She halted, began again. "For the first time since my daughter's death, I felt the desire to pray, but no words came. I do not know what to say to God after so long. You are good with words. You will know what words I should use."

He raised his eyebrows and puckered his lips, as if about to kiss someone, searching for the right words. Ethel watched him and·waited until he said, "God gives me the right words for *my* prayers, Ethel. You must ask God to give you the right words for *your* prayers."

He watched her consider this, then leaned forward and set the paper sack in her lap. "A gift for you," he said, smiling.

She opened the bag, and looked inside. "What on earth?"

"One dozen rat traps!" he replied. "Or rather – gopher traps. Bait them with carrot and set them in your rose beds."

As soon as Father John left, she took one trap in both hands, forced open the trap bar, and with her free fingers, moved the catch wire against the trigger. Thinking that it was set, she eased off, but the trap bar flung itself against her soft, white thumb, and she yelled, "Scheisse!"

Later that morning, she took five traps to Mr. Langendorf, who baited them with carrot and set them for her. She carried them from his garage to strategic locations in her rose beds.

After lunch, Ethel left her hot kitchen and sat on the porch swing. She kept the toe of one shoe pressed against the porch floor and swung herself gently with that leg, looking and listening. A cicada sang from an elm which arched over Sixth Street. A robin landed at a bird bath in Ethel's sidewalk rose bed and drank, dipped, fluttered, and flew off. A trap snapped shut, followed by a sharp squeal, and Ethel stood, nodding, her heart opening like a *Mister Lincoln*.

MAKE YOURSELF USEFUL

THE DAY I TURNED SIXTEEN, Dad took me to Jim's Sport Heaven and bought me my first rifle, a bolt-action .22 called the Remington Sharpshooter. Jim found out it was my birthday and said, "I'll throw in something any sixteen-year-old boy can use."

Dad said, "Excellent!" which is what he always said when someone threw in something for nothing.

Jim reached into the glass-top counter and pulled out a yellow cardboard box the size of an egg carton and labeled, "4 Power Telescopic Sight." He opened the box, tilted it, and slid out a black metal scope. "This mounts on your rifle barrel and magnifies your vision by four times. Black crosshairs pinpoint your aim." He held the scope up to his right eye, shut his left eye, pointed the scope toward a fly buzzing and bumping against the front screen-door behind us, and said, "That fly looks as big as a crow through this scope!"

Dad looked at me, smiled, and said to Jim, "My son's going to spend some time with my folks on the farm. Plenty of flies to shoot there." In the city, a rifle was a weapon. On the farm, a rifle was a tool, as necessary and useful as a shovel, pitchfork, or hay hook.

That afternoon, Dad helped me mount my scope and showed me how to safely load, carry, and unload the rifle, often repeating the two commandments of gun safety: "Always treat a gun as loaded. Never point it at a person – or anything you don't want to shoot."

The next morning, Dad got me up just after dawn. I put on my work jeans, white T-shirt, and Redwing work boots, and packed my dufflebag – just long enough for my new rifle. Dad put on his light gray suit, short-sleeved white shirt, and black-and-gray striped tie, and packed his black leather suitcase. We walked out of the house together, leaving mother and brother still under their blankets, asleep. Dad paused on the front porch, checked the sky for clouds, and breathed in deeply, a farm boy who still appreciated morning quiet and fresh air.

He headed his Ford Torino north out of Milwaukee. Just after crossing Cedar Creek in Cedarburg, we entered Wisconsin farm country, and Dad declared, "God's country!" We drove past red and gray barns with fieldstone foundations, past tall white frame farmhouses with big front porches, past dark green and purple-pink alfalfa fields, past walls of bright green woods and fields of cut, drying timothy, past creeks twisting their way through brushy ravines along the road – first on our right, then ducking under a culvert and appearing next on our left – past ponds ringed by stiff cattails and dotted with muskrat houses and puddle-ducks feeding, their feathered rumps pointing at the pale blue sky, their beaks probing muddy pond bottoms.

We didn't talk much, but we pointed a lot – at a red-tailed hawk on a telephone poll, a long grass snake crossing the road ahead of us, and a swath of trees downed by a recent tornado. Just outside Plymouth, Dad pointed across the divided highway at a gang of motorcyclists dressed in black leather, heading south. They rode those big Harleys, tailpipes rumbling with a sound so deep and distinctive that it carried a U.S. patent number. Dad said, "Those guys are trouble."

We passed through Elkhart Lake, turned north on Highway 67, and soon crested the hill near the farm. Dad, always happy to see his boyhood home, said, "There she is!" Even from a half mile off, you could see that the farm had been laid out to blend with each rise and dip of the land and that the buildings and fields received much care and attention. The house and barn were painted white and separated by a driveway of crushed white gravel and green lawn. Behind the house, the land rose into a drumlin – a rounded glacial hill – and was covered with piles of drying hay which looked like a village of miniature huts.

Dad signaled, slowed, and turned into the driveway, which took us through the roadside stand of basswood and maple. The tires crunched gravel, and the car passed through shafts of sunlight and tree shadows. Dad rolled down his window, took a deep breath, and said, "If heaven doesn't smell like cut alfalfa and dry sheep shit, I don't ever want to go there."

Grandpa, a short, wiry man dressed in striped bib overalls, walked out of the open tractor doors in the barn, and Dad said, "The older he gets, the more time he spends in the barn. Maybe he sleeps there now. Check it out while you're here and let me know."

Dad got out of the car and the two men shook hands, without hurry, father and son, farmer and salesman. The three of us walked side by side to the farmhouse. Grandma, a short, strong woman with thick legs, white hair, and matching apron, was putting a coffee cake and four coffee cups on the table when we walked into her kitchen.

"Have a bite," she said, smiling.

After a bit of joking and news, Dad looked at Grandma and said, "Got to go make a living. I'll be in Green Bay this week on business. I'll stop by on Monday to get him out of your hair."

She nodded, her eyes sparkling behind her silver-framed glasses.

Looking at me, Dad said, "Make yourself useful."

After seeing Dad off, Grandpa went right back to work, and I followed him to the wire sparrow-trap in the barnyard. An English sparrow, a dirty and unwelcome nuisance on the farm, fluttered inside the trap, frantic, trying to find a way out of the coiled screen. Grandpa opened the door to the trap, reached in, grabbed the sparrow, put its head under his heel, and calmly crunched its skull. He tossed the limp, feathered carcass onto a pile of barn straw.

We walked to the pasture gate, which he pushed open. As he closed the gate behind us, he reminded me, "You open a gate, you close it." You could walk out of his house and leave the door wide open in winter and he might not notice or care, but if you entered his pasture and left the gate open, he would know instantly and could think of nothing else until that gate was closed.

The pasture, grazed short by the sheep, looked like a bumpy putting green. Grandpa stopped to scrape a bit of soft manure from his shoe onto a bare spot in the pasture, and a thirteen-striped gopher chirped an alarm near us. I walked over to a tiny mound of moist soil and looked into a freshly dug tunnel.

Grandpa said, "Didn't have gophers years ago, but now I got so many you'd think I'm raising them. Not long ago one of the ewes bust her leg in a gopher hole. Hobbled back to the barn on three legs."

"She make it?" I asked.

"Yaah ... to the kitchen table. Butchered her that day."

"Can't you poison the gophers?"

"Don't like poison."

Sensing an opportunity to be useful, I said, "You want me to get rid of them for you?"

Surprised at my offer, he asked, "And how do you aim to do that?"

"With my new .22."

He looked at me and smiled, not ready to put his faith in a city boy with a brand new rifle.

"You willing to pay a bounty?" I asked.

"A bounty?"

"Nickel for each carcass."

He liked the idea of a bounty, because failure cost him nothing. He nodded, and we shook hands, sealing the deal directly over that fresh gopher hole.

Ten minutes later, I rested the barrel of my Remington Sharpshooter on the pasture gate and surveyed the sheep pasture through my scope. I spotted a gopher standing on its hind feet next to a purple thistle and laid the crosshairs across its chest. Grandpa stood alongside, curious. I took a breath, blew it out evenly between my lips, and squeezed the trigger.

Crack!

Dirt flew up at the gopher's feet.

Grandpa chuckled and said, "Well, you might have scared him to death, but you didn't hit him. I can see I ain't going to go broke paying bounties."

"An inch too low," I said, holding a cupped hand up to Grandpa. "Give me a dime."

"You got to kill two gophers before you get a dime," he said.

"I just want to borrow one."

He handed me a dime, which I used to adjust the scope's vertical mount screw. After getting his dime back, Grandpa walked off to check his hay.

I fired a box of fifty shells that morning, from all over the pasture, adjusting the scope after each shot, learning how to use my new rifle and scope. Just as I laid the crosshairs at the base of a gopher's ear, I heard a man's voice from the highway yell, "You there! What are you doing?" I eased off the trigger, turned around, and saw the Kiel cop standing behind the highway tractor gate, looking at me. His silver badge glittered in the sun and his black-and-white squad was parked behind him in the tractor lane. I put the rifle down, got up, and walked over to him.

He repeated his question, "What are you doing?"

"Making myself useful – shooting gophers."

"Who are you?"

"Adam's grandson."

"Adam's farm is within Kiel city limits now, and it's against the law to shoot off a gun within city limits. He should have told you."

"Oh!" I said, in a tone which implied, stupid me, I should have known better – I'll never do it again, Officer!

At lunch, Grandpa said grace, looked up, and asked, "Officer

Henke paid you a visit, did he?"

I nodded.

"Your first day here and already in trouble with the law," he said, chuckling. "What'd Henke want?"

"Said the farm is within city limits and that it's against the law to shoot a gun here."

Irritated, Grandpa said, "*Acch!* This is a farm, not a city! Henke ought to know that." Grandpa did not like anyone saying what could or could not be done on his farm, which he had owned and worked long before Kiel had city limits, long before Henke was born. Grandpa added. "I heard lots of shooting this morning. Must be lots of laughing gophers!"

I pointed out the kitchen window and said, "Twenty of them aren't laughing." Grandpa squinted at the gate and saw my neat row of little striped carcasses slung across the top crosspiece of the pasture gate. I added, "You owe me one dollar."

"I'll be gol-damned," he said, lifting his rear off the chair, pulling his flat, black, sweat-stained wallet from his back pocket. He took out a moist, limp dollar bill and set it on the table in front of me. "This afternoon, we'll load hay and give them gophers a rest. But tomorrow, I want you to line up some more gophers on that gate. Never mind what Henke says."

The next morning, I was back at it. With each gopher I shot, I backed farther away from the pasture – in order to improve my sharpshooting and further impress Grandpa. By Saturday, I had my rifle sighted-in for one hundred paces and was shooting from Dad's old bedroom window, upstairs in the farmhouse.

At lunch, we ate chops from the ewe which had broken her leg in the gopher hole, along with new potatoes and green beans. A warm breeze blew through the open windows and against our faces. The chickens clucked and fussed in the upstairs barn coop. The sheep, heads down, grazed the pasture between the barn and highway. A dozen barn swallows perched side by side on the telephone wire, facing us, plunging their little beaks into their orange and white breast feathers, freshening up.

All at once, the sheep stopped grazing, raised their heads, looked to the south, and listened. Like the sheep, we stopped chewing and listened.

"Thunder," I said.

"No." Grandpa said.

"What then?" I asked.

"Trouble," Grandpa said.

Grandma nodded.

"What do you mean?" I asked.

"That motorcycle gang from Milwaukee," he said. "The Outlaws."

"They come here?"

"They come through here from time to time," Grandma said.

The deep throated rumble grew louder. From my chair, I watched the Highway 67 hill. A lone biker crested the hill, followed by others. Men drove the high-handlebar bikes and women rode as passengers, their legs straddling thick chrome mufflers. The rumble vibrated my elbows against the table and sent the sheep running for the barn. The barn swallows scattered.

As the bikers got closer to the corner, they slowed but did not stop – rolling right through the stop sign as if it were meant for other people. The lead biker rode a metallic blue Harley which glittered and flashed in the sunlight. He wore dark sunglasses, blond hair to his shoulders, and black leather from skull cap to boots. Driving by, he looked toward us, as if surveying the farm.

Downshifting, the lead biker slowed, pointed at the farm, and turned across the left lane onto Grandpa's gravel tractor lane, the lane where Officer Henke had parked his squad car to question me. The other bikers slowed, put out their legs, and stopped on the highway, balancing their big bikes, watching their leader. He opened the gate latch without getting off his bike, kicked open the gate with his big boot, and drove right onto the sheep pasture.

"What on earth?" Grandma said.

Two by two, the bikers turned off the highway, came down the tractor lane, and rolled to a stop amid the gopher holes, dry sheep shit, and purple-flowered thistles. They shut off their engines and got off their bikes, until all of them – forty or fifty – stood alongside their quiet machines, stretching and talking.

The three of us glanced at one another, blinked, and looked back at the pasture, which moments ago had held a flock of grazing sheep and now held a gang of Outlaws, Milwaukee's most notorious bikers. One biker took aluminum cans out of his black saddlebags and tossed them, one by one, to others standing near him.

"They're having a beer break," I said. "Original Pabst Blue Ribbon."

Quietly, Grandpa said, "They left the gate open." Grandpa might be able to tolerate an Outlaws' beer party on his sheep pasture, but he could not tolerate that open gate. He rose from his chair.

"Adam! Where do you think you're going?" Grandma said, alarmed.

"To close the gate – and have a word with those boys."

"Sit down this instant! No telling what kind of trouble you'll get into if you bother them."

Grandpa, his eyes on the open gate, ignored his wife, left the kitchen, let the screen door bang behind him, and walked across the driveway toward the pasture. I thought, my God! He's nuts! They'll take him apart!

Grandma got up and said, "I'm calling Henke."

Grandpa, in his striped blue-and-white bibs, walked right through the gang of black-leather bikers, closed and latched the pasture gate, then turned and walked to the lead biker, a man twice his size and half his age. The biker leaned against his bike as if he owned the ground upon which he stood and watched Grandpa approach.

Behind me, Grandma spoke to the telephone operator: "Janet – You call Officer Henke on the radio right now and get him to come to our place. We got a showdown on our sheep pasture that might get ugly."

Grandpa said something to the lead biker and pointed toward the gate. Without as much as glancing at the gate, the guy set his beer can on his motorcycle seat, took a step towards Grandpa, and shoved him. Jesus! I thought. They're going to get in a fight! I ran up the stairs into Dad's old bedroom, where I could get a better view and be near my rifle.

Grandpa didn't back off and got shoved again – so hard that he went down and landed on his butt. "That does it!" I said, grabbing my Remington Sharpshooter from the corner, loading it, kneeling in front of the window, and watching the biker's every move. He stood over Grandpa, shouting and pointing at the farmhouse, trying to get rid of the pesky old man in front of him, but I knew that Grandpa would not leave.

I set the rifle barrel across the window sill and looked through the scope, laying the crosshairs on that beer can sitting on the motorcycle seat.

Aim. Steady. Exhale. *Crack!*

The beer can flew off the leather seat – end over end – and landed on the pasture grass, upright, beer flowing from the bullet hole like golden blood from a wound. Stunned, the biker looked at the beer can, and then at the farmhouse. I raised my hand and waved, so that he could see me.

When Grandpa got back on his feet, the lead biker scowled at him, wondering what to do next with this old farmer in his face. Wanting to help the guy make the right decision, I put the crosshairs on the Pabst Blue Ribbon insignia and pulled the trigger.

Crack!

The fifty-grain bullet sent the can rolling across the pasture, white foam pouring out of each bullet hole. The biker flinched and took one step back. At least I got him moving! I thought.

Grandpa, seizing the moment, walked to the highway gate, opened it, and gestured for the bikers to leave. Still, no one moved. I put the crosshairs on the can one more time.

Crack!

Child's play! The empty can flew into the air and landed on its end, this time upside-down.

The lead biker looked in my direction, raised his arm, made a fist, and slowly uncurled his middle finger until it stood straight, stiff and full of meaning. This worried me. If he still won't leave, what can I shoot next? I wondered. His tires? No. Then he can't leave!

From behind me, Grandma asked, "Are those boys getting the message?"

As if hearing her question, the lead biker turned, threw his leg across his bike, grabbed his handlebars, and kick-started his engine. He pointed toward the gate where Grandpa stood, a silent command to his troops.

"Yes," I said. "They got the message."

The Outlaws all kick-started their engines, growling them more than they had to, rolling across the pasture toward the open gate. Within a few minutes, Grandpa swung the gate shut behind the last biker. He turned and began to pick up the empty beer cans scattered across the sheep-shorn grass.

Grandma and I listened to the open-road roar of the bikes fade to a quiet low rumble, like thunder in the distance. The barn swallows flew back to the telephone wire and alighted, though this time they put their backs to us and faced the pasture. A single ewe stuck her head through the open barn door and looked at the highway. I set my rifle in the corner, turned to Grandma, and said, "Let's finish lunch, shall we?" Exuberant, I reached for her arm and escorted her down the stairs arm in arm, as if heading for the dance floor together.

In the kitchen, I pulled back her table chair. "Oh my! Such a gentleman!" she said, as she watched her husband come in from the field as she had most every day for the last forty years.

Grandpa came into the kitchen, set a Pabst Blue Ribbon can at the center of the table, and pointed at the three bullet holes. "Pretty good shooting!" he said. "For a city kid!"

And with that, we burst out laughing, laughing until Grandpa's bald head lay cupped in his sturdy hands, laughing until Grandma pulled a white hanky from her apron pocket and dabbed away tears, laughing until saw I saw Henke's black-and-white squad with red light flashing pull up the driveway.

Henke parked, got out, and stood alongside his squad, his radio in hand, his eyes searching the pasture.

"What are we going to tell Henke?" I asked, worried.

"*Nichts,*" Grandpa said.

Henke walked to the back door, pressed his face against the screen, and peered in at us. "Heard the Outlaws paid you a visit."

"Yaah!" Grandma said.

"How did you get rid of them?" Henke asked.

"I told them you were on your way," Grandpa said.

Grandma added, "Are you going to stand there all day or are you going to come in and have a little lunch?"

SMALL FORTUNES

Harry Herbst opened his eyes, stretched, and yawned on Monday morning, August 5, 1960, one month to the day after his sixtieth birthday.

A bachelor at sixty, a loner most of his life, Harry lived in a rented room with one window, pale green walls, oak floor, a maple chair with hardened glue oozing out of each joint, a bedside table piled high with library books, and an iron bed with fifty thousand dollars in uncirculated hundred-dollar bills sewn into the mattress. Each night, he slept on a small fortune – enough to buy the house he lived in as well as the house on either side, all brown and white bungalows with steep-pitched roofs lined up elbow to elbow along his street like men in uniform. He liked waking on money warmed and shaped by his body.

His paisley-print pajamas clung to his white, damp skin as Harry walked to the open window. Across the alley, a neighbor woman cut orange, red, and yellow zinnias in her garden, singing to herself, while above and behind her a white and gray cloud-mountain churned in the western sky. Harry listened for thunder and sniffed for rain. When the woman looked in his direction,

Harry ducked out of sight.

Harry had grown up in a family with money. His father had owned Herbst's Cut Flowers, a thriving Milwaukee business which had sold bouquets of fresh flowers to funeral homes, restaurants, and hotels. The Herbst family home had a bouquet of tall, fresh flowers in every room, a bedroom for each son, and a third-story turret with views of downtown Milwaukee and Lake Michigan. In 1927, on his deathbed, Harry's father had passed the business on to his oldest son, Norman. Knowing Harry's love of thrift and detail, Norman had offered his younger brother the job of book-keeper.

All bills and receipts ended up on Harry's desk, and at the end of his first month on the job, he had called his older brother into his office, closed the door, dropped a thick stack of receipts onto the scuffed oak floor at Norman's feet, and declared, "As long as I'm bookkeeper, no more company money will be used for Cuban cigars or Italian suits!" Norman nodded, not to acknowledge agreement but to admit to himself his mistake in hiring Harry.

On a warm, breezy day less than a year after that moment, Norman had invited his younger brother into his office, shut the door behind him, lit a Cuban cigar, and said, "Why stay when you're not wanted? I'll buy you out for five thousand." Hurt yet relieved, Harry had taken the money and left the family business – just as the business climate soured across Milwaukee and the country.

Unwilling to trust his cash to a bank, Harry had sewed the money into his mattress until he could decide where to invest it. In October, 1929, the stock market collapsed, and the banks closed. Herbst's Cut Flowers could no longer borrow cash, so the company wilted like a bouquet without water. Just after Thanksgiving, Norman made a final payroll and closed the business.

Norman, stripped of income and prestige, had begun to visit Harry at Harry's rented room, bringing long-stemmed carnations and boxes of chocolate as if calling on a sweetheart, saying such things as "blood is thicker than water," and "brothers to the end." Then came the requests for money, which Harry was willing to meet for the sake of Norman's wife and children. Harry would not see his brother again until Norman needed more money. Though both men knew that Norman would never repay Harry, Norman had insisted on receiving the money as "a loan."

Cash was king during the Depression, and Harry regularly raided his mattress stash and bought distressed blue-chip stocks and vacant, weed-choked city lots – for pennies on the dollar. In this way, Harry turned his cash into a small fortune of equities and real estate. As his assets grew, so did his mistrust of people who, like Norman, seemed more interested in his money than in him. Harry began to prefer the company of strangers who did not know of his wealth and treated him with simple, ordinary respect.

Harry, a black umbrella tucked under his arm, walked to the corner of 34th Street and Wisconsin Avenue and stood behind three women at the bus stop. One woman lifted her nose, sniffed, turned around, and smiled at Harry, who, convinced that women could smell money, had disguised the scent by splashing citrus cologne against his neck and cheeks. He smelled like a blooming lime tree.

Harry got off the bus at Fourth and Wisconsin and waited to cross the avenue, along with a dozen men dressed in suits, ties, and black leather shoes. When they got the green light, the men took off in long strides, eyes fixed on the finish line across the street. Harry, in his scuffed loafers, crossed behind them at his own pace, following the aroma of frying bacon into Marc's Big Boy Restaurant. He walked to an empty wood and vinyl stool at the counter and sat. A tall, slender waitress no more than thirty years old appeared in front of him as if summoned, turned over his white cup, poured black coffee, and asked, "The usual?"

Harry nodded and smiled at her, whom he knew only as Wendy. He loved to watch her move through the crowded restaurant, pouring coffee, balancing plates, nodding, spinning, dodging, scribbling, the breakfast ballet of a working woman – with an audience of one man who knew that women were for other men, not him.

Wendy placed a folded *Wall Street Journal* alongside Harry's coffee cup, and he nodded at her again and began to read a back-page story entitled, "Wisconsin Gas & Electric Seeks Rate Hike." Harry knew the rate hike would put more money in his pocket by raising the price of the stock. He owned ten lots – a thousand shares. Wendy delivered his breakfast plate of bacon, two eggs up, and white-bread toast. He looked at her and said, "Your heating bill will be higher this winter."

"Just what I need," she said.

After breakfast, Harry left Marc's and walked east on Wisconsin, entering a lobby paneled in walnut, with an oil painting of a Great Lakes sailing vessel hung on each wall. Harry took his place in a group of men who stood around the ticker tape, a polished-steel machine under a glass globe. "WGE 35 1/2" appeared on the tape and he thought, up a dollar-fifty on news of that rate hike. Without averting his eyes from the tape, Harry leaned toward the man to his left and said, "Looks like a good day for the utilities."

"So far, so good," the man said.

"Radio said rain by afternoon," Harry added.

Another man said, "Don't believe it. If rain was coming, my knees would be killing me."

Over the next hour, Harry spoke about the weather, world news, and business trends without ever looking away from the tape. At one point, James Wenzel, Harry's stockbroker, walked up to Harry, pressed a cup of coffee into Harry's hand, and stood elbow to elbow with Harry for several minutes, his way of letting Harry know that he was available for making trades. Harry used Wenzel for buying and selling, but he did not use Wenzel for advice, preferring to do his own research and pick his own stocks.

Harry left the Dean Witter office at eleven o'clock, and as soon as he walked onto the sidewalk, a fat raindrop splattered against his bald scalp. He looked up. Dark clouds hung above the dirty brick buildings, and Harry raised and opened his umbrella. His feet ached from standing all morning, but he walked lightly since his portfolio was plus two thousand for the day, and he looked forward to spending a long afternoon at the city library. There, Harry would do as he did each afternoon: doze, read *The New York Times*, doze, study company fundamentals in the dark blue, spiral-bound volumes of *Value Line*, doze.

As he walked along the Wisconsin Avenue sidewalk, Harry got in an argument with himself about one of his holdings. Raindrops splashed against his umbrella and the pavement.

Call Wenzel this afternoon. Sell WG&E on strength. Lock in your profits, he told himself.

By the time he got to Fourth Street, the pavement was wet and steaming, and Harry pulled his umbrella closer to his head. He stepped onto the Wisconsin Avenue crosswalk behind a business-man who held a folded newspaper over his head.

No! Harry told himself. Don't call Wenzel. Don't sell WG&E. Hold your position....

The sound of rubber skidding against wet pavement caused Harry to look to his left. A 1959 powder-blue Chevrolet Impala, tires locked, skidded towards him. He glimpsed the face of the driver, a woman about his age, her soft, pink tongue sticking out between her clenched, red lips. Harry had no time to move or fear. He calmly thought, I'm probably the first person she's ever killed.

"Mr. Herbst? Can you hear me?" Harry opened his eyes and saw a woman in a white dress and cap standing over him, her blonde hair backlit by an overhead light.

Groggy, Harry asked, "Are you an angel?"

"No. I'm your nurse. Alice Denmann."

"Where am I?"

"Deaconess Hospital."

"What happened?"

"You walked right into traffic on Wisconsin Avenue."

A throb of pain shot down the left side of Harry's body, jarring loose the memory of the woman's face in the powder-blue Im-pala. He reached down to touch his left leg but could not feel it. "My leg! Where is my leg?"

The nurse took Harry's hand and placed it against his foot-to-hip cast. "Your leg is inside this cast, Mr. Herbst."

"What's wrong with my leg?"

"Broken in three places."

"How long will I be here?"

"Till we can get you on crutches."

Harry frowned as he slid his hand between his legs. "What's this?"

"A catheter. You can urinate without getting out of bed."

"Oh."

"Is there someone you'd like us to notify?"

Harry shook his head. His parents were dead. He hadn't seen his brother, Norman, in twenty years. And he had no friends. Exhausted, he closed his eyes and slept until the next morning, when he was awakened by a burning and tugging between his legs. He opened his eyes, and Nurse Denmann held up the end of the catheter, which she had just pulled from his penis, and smiled.

"You're no angel, that's for sure," Harry said.

"Ring me when you need to go."

Harry looked at the bathroom across the room and said, "I'll manage myself."

"No, you won't. You'll need help at home, too."

"I live alone."

"That won't do, Mr. Herbst."

Harry, incredulous, looked at her and said, "That will have to do."

An orderly delivered Harry's breakfast, ending their conversation.

After his breakfast, Harry tried to get up without the help of his nurse. He slid his cast to the edge of his mattress and it dropped to the floor, lifting his torso as if it were the other end of a teeter-totter. He winced and pressed his eyelids together, waiting for the pain to pass. A pair of warm hands touched his shoulders, steadying him. A woman's voice he knew said, "Harry, take it easy."

He opened his eyes. "Wendy! How did you know I was here?"

"We heard sirens and found out that a pedestrian got hit on the avenue. Our manager went to check, told me it was you."

A woman dressed in black appeared in the doorway behind Wendy. She gripped a large black purse with both hands, and her pink cheeks and red lips twitched, signaling her discomfort.

Harry recognized the woman, his eyes widening with alarm.

Wendy, protective of her patron, turned and asked, "Who are you?"

"My name is Blanche Patterson."

Wendy turned to Harry. "You know this woman?"

"Not exactly."

Nurse Denmann came into the room. She glanced at Harry's face, sized up the other women, and asked, "Are you okay, Harry?"

Harry's room was suddenly full of women eager to help him and suspicious of one another. All three women began to talk at once, introducing themselves, explaining why they had come, gathering in a tight circle at the foot of Harry's bed.

Harry tried to get up without being noticed by the women, but suddenly six soft hands closed around his arms like padded claws and helped him to his feet. Wendy asked, "Where do you think you're going?"

Harry, out of breath, stared at the bathroom.

With the help of the women and a pair of crutches, Harry got to the bathroom door, where he turned and said, "Why don't you all go to the cafeteria for a cup of coffee and get better acquainted."

Which is exactly what they did.

Twenty minutes later, the women returned to Harry's room and stood hip to hip at the foot of his bed, which he had managed to get back into by himself. He could see that they no longer mistrusted one another, that they had, in fact, joined ranks.

Nurse Denmann announced, "We have a plan."

Harry said nothing, but he began to worry.

"We know you live alone," Nurse Denmann said, "And that you have no family. But you're going to need help once you leave here."

Harry, his leg still aching from his trip to the toilet, could no longer protest her assessment.

The nurse turned to the woman who had struck Harry and added, "Blanche Patterson lives alone, too. She's offered to put you up in her home and take care of you until you're better able to get around."

This thought did not sit well with Harry. He looked at his nurse and said, "No."

Nurse Denmann said, "If you have a better idea, Mr. Herbst, we'd love to hear it."

"I'll stay right here until I can get around better."

Wendy knew firsthand of Harry's thrift and said, "This bed costs you three hundred a day, Harry."

"I have Mutual of Omaha."

Shaking her head, Nurse Denmann added, "No insurance pays for unnecessary hospital days."

Harry clenched his lips, thinking. He looked at Wendy and said, "Well, maybe I can stay with you."

She smiled and shook her head. "I got two bedrooms at home,

Harry, with a husband in one and two kids in the other. Besides, I work all day, remember?"

Harry folded his arms across his chest, stymied.

Blanche Patterson stepped forward and said, "Mr. Herbst. I feel awful about the accident –"

"Not as awful as I feel," Harry said, interrupting her, angry that she had come. He crossed his arms across his chest.

"Of course not, Mr. Herbst," she said, stepping back, closing her mouth, bowing her head, surrendering to his suffering.

Harry watched her and softened. "I'm sorry, Mrs. Patterson," he said. "There was nothing you could have done. I walked right in front of your car."

Blanche smiled weakly, and said, "The offer to stay with me still stands, Mr. Herbst. In allowing me to help you, you'd be helping me."

Two days later, Harry got released from the hospital. He sat in a wheelchair outside the front door of the hospital, Nurse Denmann behind him. Blanche pulled her powder-blue Impala into the hospital entrance, the car's chrome bumper and grill gleaming in the hot August sun. Harry closed his eyes, recalling the accident.

He tried to get into the front seat, but he could only get his body or his cast – not both – into the car. "This isn't working," he said. "Let's try the back seat." He backed in this time, sat on the seat, and Blanche and the nurse got in from the other side, grabbed his belt, and pulled him across the seat until both he and his cast were in the car.

Nurse Denmann looked at Harry and said, "Goodbye, Mr. Herbst." She closed the car door, turned to Blanche, and added,

"My work is done. Yours is just beginning."

From the back seat, Harry studied Blanche's silver hair and pale neck. "I can see you are a cautious driver, Mrs. Patterson."

She glanced at him in her rearview mirror.

"Where do you live?" he asked.

"Lake Drive."

Surprised, Harry thought, she must have money! This thought put Harry at ease. He turned, rolled down the window, felt the warm wind against his face, and watched the cars and buses go by.

Blanche slowed, put on her left turn signal, and turned onto a paved driveway which led to a stone house half-hidden by oaks and maples, an English Tudor home with leaded windows and dark brown shutters. Its elegance reminded Harry of his family home.

Blanche stopped her car, put it in park, set the emergency brake, turned off the ignition, and looked at Harry in her rearview mirror. "Since my husband passed, I live upstairs, except to cook and eat. You'll have the downstairs pretty much to yourself."

"One room is all I need," Harry said, a bit nervous about having a whole floor to call his own.

Blanche got out and helped Harry onto his crutches. By the time they reached the front door, Harry was out of breath, so Blanche pushed open the heavy door, seated him on a loveseat just inside the entryway, and sat beside him as he caught his breath.

"Do you like to read, Mr. Herbst?" she asked, pointing to a large room with floor-to-ceiling bookcases and books. "The library was my husband's pride and joy. Now, let me show you to your room."

Blanche set up a card table and two chairs in the library so that

Harry would not have to walk far for meals, and she served lunch: egg-salad sandwiches, bite-sized and cut into perfect triangles.

During lunch, Harry asked, "What kinds of books are in your library, Mrs. Patterson?"

"The Classics. History. My husband taught Greek and Latin at Marquette University."

After a long silence, Blanche asked, "Are you retired, Mr. Herbst?"

Harry nodded.

"Do you have any family still living?"

"A brother." Harry shrugged his shoulders and added, "Haven't seen him in twenty years."

Blanche realized that Harry was not used to receiving personal questions, so she changed the subject.

That evening, Harry lay on his bed, reading a book written by Blanche's husband entitled *The Ancient Greeks*, but when Blanche walked past his closed door, he set the book on his chest and listened. She locked the front door, climbed the stairs, and walked into her bedroom, which was directly above Harry's room. She opened and shut a bureau drawer, and a minute later, flushed the toilet and clicked off the lights. Her mattress compressed and crinkled as she lay down for the night.

The next morning, Blanche and Harry sat across from one another at the card table in the library, each holding a cup of coffee, their knees nearly touching under the table. Harry asked, "Mrs. Patterson, do you ever get lonely?"

She looked at her guest, smiled, and said, "Yes." After a sip of coffee, she returned the question, "And you, Mr. Herbst?"

The doorbell rang before Harry could answer.

"Who on earth could that be?" Blanche asked. She opened the front door and asked, "May I help you?"

"Is this the Patterson residence?"

Harry recognized the voice at once.

"Yes," said Blanche.

"I'm Harry's brother, Norman."

"Oh, my! Come in, Mr. Herbst."

Eager to greet his brother, Harry grabbed his crutches and stood, but then he thought, Norman must need money. Harry's good leg began to quiver, as if about to give way, and he sat.

Norman walked into the library and stopped. Both men nodded, uncertain what to say to one another after so long.

Blanche said, "Mr. Herbst, please have a seat, I'll get you some coffee."

Norman sat in Blanche's chair and the two brothers studied each other.

"How did you find me?" Harry asked.

"Nurse Denmann phoned me, told me what happened and where I'd find you."

"That nurse can't keep her nose out of my life."

Blanche brought in a cup of coffee, set it on the card table in front of Norman, and said, "You two visit. I'll be in the kitchen."

"You look well taken care of," Norman said, sizing up his brother.

"Why have you come?" Harry asked.

Norman looked down, hesitating before he answered.

Harry asked, "How much do you need?"

Norman reached into the chest pocket of his sportscoat, pulled out a white envelope, and set it on the card table between them.

Puzzled, Harry looked at the envelope.

"For you," Norman said.

Harry pulled the envelope to him, opened it, and saw a thin stack of hundred dollar bills.

"I'm paying off some old debts, Harry…. It's my way of saying, 'Let's put those times behind us and start out fresh, while we still got a little time.'"

Astonished, Harry leaned back in his chair and looked at his brother.

Blanche, having overheard the conversation from the kitchen, walked into the library and said, "Gentlemen. I'm in the mood to have a dinner party this Saturday. Mr. Herbst, are you free?"

Norman nodded.

"Are you married?"

Norman nodded again.

"Bring your wife." Turning to Harry, she added, "You think about the friends you'd like to invite."

Harry thought, friends?

Blanche turned to the dining room and looked at the walnut table which she dusted each week but hadn't used since winter. "I'm having a vision," she said. "I'm seeing a prime rib … pink at the center, with fresh green beans, stuffed potatoes … oh, and what's that? Oh, my … the lovely and gracious hostess, Mrs. Patterson, is placing a peach pie on the table for dessert." She turned to the men and asked, "Would that be satisfactory?"

Both men glanced at one another and nodded.

"Splendid!" Blanche said, the joy of a girl in her voice.

Harry thought, this woman invents life as she goes – that's what keeps her young.

That evening, Harry did not sleep well. He had three disturb-
ing dreams about the old family business, and one very pleasant
dream about Blanche. In that dream, he had climbed the dark
stairs on two sound legs, stood in the open doorway of Blanche's
bedroom, and watched her sleep, the warm, yellow streetlight
pouring through her front window and illuminating her peaceful
face.

On Saturday, Harry awakened in the dark, rose to his elbows,
and listened. Someone shut a kitchen cupboard and turned on
the faucet. Curious, Harry got up, grabbed his crutches, and made
his way down the dark hallway, wearing only his paisley-print
pajamas. Peering into the bright kitchen, Harry saw Blanche standing at the kitchen sink with her back to him, still dressed in her
pink robe and slippers. Harry turned around for a quiet retreat
but accidentally banged a crutch against the door frame.

Blanche jumped and turned. "Mr. Herbst!"

Harry stopped and turned toward her, careful to keep his eyes
on the linoleum floor, his face – and bare scalp – blushing pink.

"Haven't you ever seen a woman in a robe?" she asked.

"No."

Charmed by his shyness, she said. "And no woman has ever
seen you in your pajamas?"

"No."

Blanche laughed out loud. "You have lived through the Great
Depression and two World Wars, Mr. Herbst. You'll live through
this, too."

Harry looked up at her and grinned, enjoying the awkward
moment for the first time.

"Now get over here right now and scrub these potatoes,"

Blanche ordered. It was the first time she had invited him to assist with housework.

Harry got to the sink, set his crutches against the counter, and grabbed a fat, mud-crusted potato.

Blanche stepped alongside him, her hip pressing against his hip, her shoulder pressing against his as she handed him a vegetable brush. He stopped breathing and felt a trickle of blood rush to his groin, but he stayed focused on the task at hand, turning on the faucet, holding the potato under the rush of warm water, and brushing the mud off the thick, gnarled skin.

For the next three hours, Harry assisted Blanche in the kitchen, he in his pajamas, she in her robe. When the stores opened, Blanche got dressed and went grocery shopping. Harry got dressed, phoned Milwaukee Floral Displays — a one-time competitor of Herbst's Cut Flowers — and asked, "You got some nice pink glads? Good. I want two dozen, delivered today."

That evening, Harry dressed himself in a Harris tweed sportscoat, which had once belonged to Blanche's husband, and sat on the entryway loveseat, his crutches alongside him. He rose and greeted the dinner guests as they arrived: first, Norman, dressed in a tuxedo, and his wife, Esther, dressed in a formal black gown. Harry glanced at himself in the tweed sportscoat and thought, I've been underdressed all day.

Then the guests Harry had invited: first, Wendy, who wore a sequined red dress with a plunging neckline, and her husband, a tall, big-armed meat cutter named Sammy, who wore a gold turtleneck and a polyester green sportscoat, the team colors of the Green Bay Packers. Next: Nurse Denmann, who arrived alone in a clingy dark dress, black stockings, and high heels. Harry, used to seeing her in her white uniform, hardly recognized her. Last: James Wenzel, Harry's stockbroker, dressed in a navy pinstripe suit, white shirt, and shiny silk tie, accompanied by a handsome, impeccably-dressed man whom Wenzel introduced as his friend, William.

The guests, strangers to one another, gathered in the library, looking at the books rather than speaking to one another, until Blanche brought in a silver platter of martinis. James Wenzel sipped his martini and said to Blanche, "Harry's awfully shy. How did you come to meet him?"

"Well, I just sort of ran into him," she said, smiling.

Blanche seated her guests at the dining-room table, placing herself and Harry at each end, with a magnum bottle of California burgundy in front of Harry. A tall bouquet of pink gladiolas stood at the table's center, their stems bunched together in a crystal vase like soft, slender logs, their flowered spikes reaching almost to the glass chandelier and arching out toward each guest. Harry leaned toward his brother and said, "The last time I remember a meal like this, you and I were just kids at the table."

Norman said, "It's good to see you again, brother."

Ten days later, Blanche drove Harry across town to his place. He was still on crutches, but he had learned to use them well, and he was eager to get back to his routine.

"That's it," Harry said, pointing to the house in which he lived.

Blanche signaled, pulled her Impala alongside the curb, put it in park, and shut off the ignition.

"I just have one room, Mrs. Patterson. Upstairs, in back."

Blanche put her warm right hand across the top of Harry's left hand and said, "Thank you, Mr. Herbst, for receiving my care.

I no longer have nightmares about the accident."

"Nor do I, Mrs. Patterson." Harry did not tell her about the dreams he had each night, sweet dreams about her, dressed in her robe. He did, however, get up the courage to ask, "May I take you to dinner sometime?"

"You may," she said.

Harry swung open the door to his room and hefted his suitcase onto the bed. He carefully put the envelope of money he had received from Norman inside the cut in his mattress, feeling around to make sure that the rest of his cash was still there. He turned and ambled to the window.

The neighbor woman was cutting the last of the zinnias in her garden, and when she looked in Harry's direction, he waved, and she waved to him. The sky above was as blue as Blanche's Impala, with one pale, wispy cloud drifting east, toward the lake.

THE GIANT

WHEN I WAS A GIRL, I WATCHED HIM from the east window of my upstairs bedroom. On summer evenings, he walked down the dirt path to the pond, his bamboo pole quivering in his hand like a long whip, a tin bucket full of earth and worms hanging from his belt. Pa stocked our pond with bluegills, and Pa didn't let anyone fish it except me, our cousins, and him. Once, I ran downstairs and shouted, "He's fishing in our pond again!"

"Leave him be, Donna," Pa said.

"Something is wrong with him."

"He's just slow."

"He's a giant!"

"*Acch!* Giants are as tall as the barn and live in fairytales, not next door."

For the most part, people tried to leave him be. Grownups greeted him with smiles and nods but kept their children away from him. My friends and I kept our distance from him, made faces behind his back, and made up stories about him. My cousin, Carl, once said, "Donna, I seen him catch a big fat bluegill in your pond, take it off his hook, hold it up by the tail like this, tilt back his head, and drop it into his mouth – whole and wiggling!"

"You lie!" I said, but I believed him.

On Saturdays, he walked along the gravel road to Gills Rock, picked up a few things at the store, and stopped at the Rock Tap, a gathering place for Lake Michigan fishermen like Pa who kept their boats at the dock. Once, I was at the Rock Tap, sitting on a bar stool next to Pa, looking out over the ferry dock, at fishing boats and the dark, rolling waves of Lake Michigan, when the giant came in. He liked being around fishermen, because, I think, they accepted him as a man, not a freak.

Pa turned and said, "Hello, Johnny!"

Johnny smiled, nodded, clomped across the wooden floor in his size-fifteen boots, and sat on the other side of Pa, who at six-two and two hundred pounds was bigger than most men. Even seated on a stool, Johnny was a full head taller than Pa – a big, square head of wind-tossed, strawberry-blond hair, with the bright, blue eyes of a boy and the rotted teeth of an old man. His chest, shoulders, and neck looked like the front half of the Detmer's Brown Swiss bull, which they had named Bulldog. Once, Carl and I were watching Mr. Detmer tend his bull, and it whirled, charged, and flattened him, the back of Detmer's head hitting the ground so hard that I thought it was going to split open like a melon dropped on concrete. He crawled out of Bulldog's pen with two busted ribs and a concussion.

Johnny's hands reminded me of nothing I'd ever seen: pink, deep wrinkles of soft flesh in between white callouses and dirt, newborn-tender and man-tough at once. When he wrapped his hand around a beer glass, the glass looked like a miniature in my doll set, and I thought, if he stuck his big ugly thumb in that glass, it would get stuck and never come out! His hands were respected by the fishermen, not for their size, but for their finesse and skill with wood. Pa said Johnny could cut, carve, steam, shape, and fasten wood better than anyone on the Door County Peninsula, and he hired Johnny for jobs that he didn't have the patience or skill to do himself, like carving a new bowstem for his fishing boat, or straightening a warped wooden wheel on our hay wagon. Pa said Johnny used only a few simple hand-tools, too – all hand-forged in Sweden, all brought to America by Johnny's Pa.

Johnny's Pa, Erik Lundeen, and his Ma, Greta, sailed from Sweden to New York on their honeymoon, traveled by rail to Wisconsin, and bought the farm to the east of my folks. Erik built the big square two-story farmhouse where Johnny and his brother were born and raised, and where Johnny lived most of his life. The Lundeen place was the northernmost farm in Door County, the last farm before woods took over the narrowing, twisting peninsula which ended at Death's Door, a treacherous stretch of Lake Michigan between the Door Peninsula and Washington Island. When I first heard the story of St. Christopher, the giant of old who ferried travelers across a deep river on his shoulders, I began to wonder if Johnny might be tall enough to walk across Death's Door with travelers on his shoulders, a ferry built of flesh and blood.

My first year in school, Erik Lundeen got pneumonia and fell off his milking stool onto the barn floor, dead. A few months after that, Greta "died of a broken heart." Johnny's only brother, Gustav, and his wife, Emma, moved back into the old farmhouse and tried to look after Johnny, but it didn't work out, and they asked Johnny to leave. I didn't blame them. I figured, why would any woman want a lout of a brother-in-law like him in her house?

Johnny, now unwelcome in his own home, got busy. He took his axe and some food and walked into the woods north of their farm. For days we heard him working, the *chunk, chunk, chunk* of his axe blade against a tree trunk, the trunk cracking and crashing against the forest floor. One morning, I looked out my bedroom window and saw Johnny leading our old Belgian mare, Lady, across our backyard, toward the woods. I ran downstairs, found Pa, and shouted, "Johnny stole Lady!"

"Johnny is borrowing Lady."

"What's he going to do with her?"

"Pull some logs out of the woods."

"He better not hurt her!"

Johnny and Lady pulled dozens of logs out of the woods, and from my upstairs bedroom window, I watched him square, notch, and raise those logs with his bare hands and his pa's tools. In a matter of weeks, he had a one-room cabin just up the hill from our pond. He made that his home and workshop and quit visiting his brother and sister-in-law. Once, when my cousin Carl was visiting me, I took him to my upstairs window and showed him Johnny's new cabin. The blood drained out of Carl's face.

"What's wrong?" I asked.

"The giant is on his own now. Nobody to watch him. He can roam the woods and roads at night like a big old mean bear." Carl was afraid of him, too.

One night, not long after Johnny moved into his cabin, I woke up from my sleep and heard a warbly, forlorn sound. I got up, walked to my open window, and saw a square of yellow light shining from the window of his cabin. Again I heard the sound, and thought, it's coming from his cabin! A woman is in there, and she's crying! I got back in bed and put the pillow over my head.

The next morning at breakfast, I was trying to figure out whether I'd had a bad dream or had actually heard a woman crying in Johnny's cabin, when Ma said, "Johnny played his fiddle last night." That's when I learned that he loved to play the fiddle, though he was never any good at it. When the wind was out of the east at night and my bedroom window was open, I could hear him tuning and playing odd, slow melodies, none of which I recognized. I thought, maybe they're Swedish songs. Maybe he makes them up.

I tried to imagine a tiny, delicate fiddle in his huge hands. So far as I knew, Johnny never went to school past the third grade, never held a regular job, never went on a date, never went to church, never had a real friend — unless you counted his big black dog, Champ. Whatever Johnny told Champ to do, he did. If Johnny had told Champ to eat me, that dog would have gobbled me up. Sometimes, Champ howled when Johnny played his fiddle.

The winter I turned ten, Ma and I took cookies to all the shut-ins just before Christmas. She drove the car, and I delivered a box of cookies to each old person and said, "Merry Christmas!" I liked my job, until Ma pulled onto the grass lane heading up to Johnny's cabin. She stopped the car just outside his cabin. Smoke rose from the tin chimney, and Champ barked like mad just inside the door. Mom smiled and said, "Johnny gets the last can of cookies."

Mother has lost her mind! I thought. I folded my arms across my chest and said, "I'd rather take cookies to the Devil in hell!"

"How you talk, girl!"

The front door opened and Johnny's body filled the doorway

from top to bottom and side to side. His dog squeezed between his legs and charged the car, barking, circling, looking for a way to get at us. Johnny yelled "Champ!" and pointed to the cabin, and the dog skulked to the open doorway, turned, sat, and watched us, silent.

Johnny walked to my window, and in an unexpected gesture, he dropped to his knees on the frozen ground so that he could see our faces. He tilted his head, as if questioning why we had come.

Ma waved at him and said to me, "Roll down your window and give him the cookies."

"No."

She reached across my lap and rolled down my window herself, shouting, "Hello there, Johnny! My daughter has something for you."

I didn't move, but my whole body trembled, and if I had been a few years younger, I'd have peed all over the car seat. Ma grabbed the cookie tin out of my hands and offered it to Johnny through my open window. He took it, lifted the cover, peeked, and smiled, his rotted teeth showing between his lips.

"Thank you, Miss Donna."

Appalled, I thought, the giant knows my name!

Ma said, "Merry Christmas, Johnny."

A few days later, I invited my girlfriends over for a skating party on our bluegill pond. Pa built us a warming fire. Ma brought us hot milk and chocolate chip cookies, and we skated and played Crack the Whip until our ankles cried out, stop! No more! Everything was going great until my best friend, Martha, screamed and pointed up the hill toward Johnny's cabin. Johnny stood at the top of the hill, watching us. His long black coat flapped against his knees in the stiff breeze, and his brown scarf, wrapped three or four times around his bull neck, whipped like a flag in the wind. When he saw us looking at him, he pulled one bare hand out of his coat pocket and held it up like an Indian chief – a greeting, I suppose, but we took it as a warning. Without another word, we all skated off the pond and ran as best we could across the snow and into the back hall, our skate blades clomping against the pine boards like cow hooves on a wooden barn floor. Ma appeared at the top of the back stairs and asked, "What's wrong?"

"The giant is watching us!" I shouted, out of breath. "Make him go away!"

Alarmed, Ma walked to the kitchen window to see for herself, and we all followed her, our skate blades denting and gouging the dark yellow linoleum. He was gone.

"Why would he watch us like that?" I asked.

"He was probably lonely and wanted to watch you girls play. Now take off those skates or get back outside!"

The next week, a winter thaw hit us, and the temperature rose to sixty during the afternoons. The snow melted, creating trickles and puddles and soggy ground. One afternoon during that thaw, I grabbed my skates and walked to the pond, which glimmered in the bright sun. Lady stood in the barnyard, broadside to the sun, one back leg raised and bent, eyes closed, eighteen hundred pounds of over-the-hill horse flesh soaking up the sun.

I put on my skates and stepped onto the ice, which was still smooth and hard, and glided above the bluegills finning in the water below, hands clasped behind my back, enjoying the warm air and sun against my face. Without warning, the ice gave way under me, and I went down like a rock, so quick that I didn't even get a gulp of air before I was under, my eyes and mouth wide open in the frigid water, my body clutching against the cold. My first thought: I'm rising! But a moment later, I looked up toward the light, got my bearings, and thought, no! I'm still going down! My winter clothes are weighing me down! I tore at my coat buttons just as my skates blades hit sand, and I bent and shoved off the bottom.

My head broke the surface and I gulped air, but before I could yell or grab the edge of the ice, I went under again. This time, I got my coat off while going down just as my skates hit sand, and I shoved off with all my might, leaving my coat on the bottom.

My head broke water a second time, and there was Johnny, kneeling on the ice, reaching for me with those pink and white hands. He missed me. I went down again, but not as far, and I kicked my way to the surface, my legs cramping, my hands and arms breaking the surface first. I felt Johnny's hand close around my wrist, and he pulled me up, but just as my head and shoulders came out of the water, the ice broke under him.

I kicked and thrashed and kept my head above water, but Johnny went under. I turned around, looking for his head. "Help!" I shouted, just as I felt a push from below with such strength that my whole body left the water as if fired from a cannon, and I landed on the ice five feet from the hole. Turning, I still could not see him. Unable to stand, I slid on my belly across the ice to the bank, got to my knees, and yelled at the house, "Help!"

Pa threw open the back door and sprinted across the backyard, Ma right behind him. When he got to me, I yelled, "Johnny saved me!" That was the first time I had ever spoken his name out loud. Pointing toward the hole in the ice, I yelled, "He's still in there!"

Pa gave me to Ma, turned, ran onto the ice, fell to his belly, and wiggled his way to the edge of the hole. He looked into the dark water and yelled, "I can't see him!" For several moments – which seemed like minutes – Pa searched the water, finally plunging his head under for a better look. Jerking his head out of the water, Pa shouted, "He's standing on the bottom, looking up at me." Pa took a big breath, pulled his chest over the hole, and plunged his head, shoulders, and right arm into the water. Oh no! I thought, he'll go in, too!

When Pa's face came out of the water, he shouted, "I got him!" Grunting and pulling, he got Johnny's head to the surface, Johnny's red hair plastered against his square skull, his mouth and eyes open. Ma and I scrambled onto the ice, eager to help. We dropped to our knees and grabbed Pa's legs, but it only took a moment to realize that even the three of us did not have the strength or leverage to get Johnny out of the pond. Pa yelled, "Donna! Get Lady! And a rope!"

My legs and arms felt locked in place by the cold, but I managed to stand, skate stiff-legged to the pond's edge, and stumble across the backyard to the barn. Lady watched me. I grabbed a coil of rope off the barn wall and searched for a bridle. Not seeing one, I walked to Lady, reached up, and pinched her soft upper lip between my thumb and forefinger with such authority that she followed me out of the barn and to the pond like Champ followed Johnny.

At pond's edge, I threw the rope across Lady's blonde mane and tied it around her neck while Ma took the other end out onto the ice and tossed it to Pa, who had his arm around Johnny's neck. He worked the rope under Johnny's limp arm, around his back, under his other arm, and knotted the rope. Turning his head, Pa backed away from the hole and shouted, "Get up!"

The sharp command startled Lady. Pa had not used her for work since he had gotten his first John Deere tractor in '46, so Lady had not heard a work command from him in five years. She snorted, twice, and turned her head toward him.

Again, he yelled, "Get up!"

Lady stepped forward until the rope grew taut, but then she halted, unaccustomed to a bare rope biting into her neck. I grabbed her soft upper lip between my fingers, pinched, and got her moving again, and Johnny's body came up out of the water and slid onto the ice like a five-hundred-pound sack of potatoes, which is probably how much he weighed in his soaking-wet winter clothes.

Pa yelled, "Ho!"

Lady halted.

Pa straddled Johnny and pressed down with both hands against his chest. Water gurgled out both sides of Johnny's open mouth. Pa let off and pressed again. More water, a grunt, a cough.

Ma helped me back to the house and drew a hot bath. I tried to undress myself but my fingers were so cold that I could not unbutton my blouse, so Ma undressed me and eased me into the hot water. After ten minutes, I could wiggle my fingers and toes, so she helped me out of the tub, dried me off, and put me to bed under every quilt in the house.

"What happened to Johnny?" I asked.

"Your father is tending him."

An hour later, Pa came into my room, smiled, and sat on my bed. "You alright?" he asked.

"No. I'm melting under this load of quilts!"

He chuckled, relieved.

"How is Johnny?"

"I got him undressed, put him to bed, and fed his cast-iron stove till the belly glowed red."

"Will he be alright?"

"I don't see why not. He's strong as an ox."

Later that afternoon, Pa checked on Johnny and visited the Lundeen Place to tell Gustav and Emma what had happened. Pa came back home upset, and I overheard him talking to Ma. "I told them that Johnny might need some looking after, but Gustav said, 'We don't have anything to do with Johnny any more, not after he tried to have his way with my wife.'"

Ma was silent for a minute and said, "So that's what happened.... Well, I'll look in on him. Somebody has to."

The next morning at the breakfast table, Ma studied my face, laid the palm of her hand across my forehead, and said to Pa, "She seems fine."

Pa asked me, "You feel okay?"

I nodded, turned to Ma and said, "I'm going with you today."

"Where?" she asked, surprised.

"To look in on Johnny."

Pa left to make repairs on his boat, and Ma and I fried up a batch of eggs and ham — more than the three of us had eaten — and packed a basket, which I insisted on carrying.

We walked across our backyard and down to the bluegill pond, pausing along the bank. The hole in the ice where I had gone down was filled with chunks of ice. A stiff, warm breeze blew across the pond, rippling the dark water, blowing the ice chunks across the hole the way the summer breeze blew our plastic bobbers across the pond's surface. My body shivered. Ma put her arm around me and said, "I'm so glad you're safe and sound."

We walked up the hill to Johnny's cabin and came upon him standing in front of his cabin, wearing nothing but his red union-suit which was stained dark with sweat under his arms, his hands clutching an axe handle, his bare, white, size-fifteen feet spread and braced against the ground. A pile of split maple lay in front of him. Champ stepped into the cabin doorway and growled at us, and Johnny looked up. He raised his eyebrows when he saw his two female neighbors staring at him in his underwear. Dropping the axe, he put his hand over his mouth like a surprised boy, turned, and lumbered into his cabin in such a hurry that he banged his big toe against the door sill. We stayed put.

He came back out, favoring his one foot, wearing the long black coat which covered up all of his union-suit except from the knees down, and I thought, that's the coat he wore to the bottom of the pond! Champ growled again, and both Ma and I took a step back. Johnny turned to his dog and shouted, "Shut up!" and immediately, he began to cough, a dry, rasping cough. Turning back to us, he added, "Sorry. My dog and me ain't used to visitors."

"Thank you for saving my daughter," Ma said.

She put her hand on my back and gently pushed me forward. I walked toward him but kept my eyes on the ground, afraid to look at him. I set the basket on the brown grass near his filthy toes and curled toenails, and backed away. He dropped to his knees as he had when we'd taken him cookies at Christmas. He looked down at the basket, lifted the red-and-white checked cloth, and took a breath through his nostrils. "Ham and eggs!" Looking at me, he said, "Thanks, Miss Donna."

I turned and ran back to Ma, who grabbed my hand and before turning to leave, said, "You need anything, Johnny, anything at all, you let us know."

At dinner that evening, Pa asked Ma, "Visit Johnny today?"

She nodded.

"How is he?"

"Seemed fine, except for a cough."

With pride, I added, "We took him a breakfast big enough to cure any cough!"

The next morning was the Sabbath. We went to church as usual, and the minister, Reverend Sturdevent, a short, chubby man who stood only one head taller than his pulpit, said, "Let us offer our prayers to God." I closed my eyes and tried to pray but could think of nothing but going down in that dark water, so I opened my eyes and looked around.

As usual, people began to speak up, mostly old women, one after the other, praying for this or that as if they were standing in line at the butcher shop and calling out their meat orders. Mrs. Frances Elderberry prayed for the tumor in her stomach, that God might make it shrink and go away. Mrs. Elaine Orth prayed for her wayward sister in Milwaukee, that she might come to know the Lord Jesus. Mrs. Olsa prayed for her husband, that his bad back might get better so that he could work again and get out from under her feet.

Like most of the men who came to church, Pa never spoke or sang or even opened his mouth during worship, so he startled me by laying his hand on mine and saying, in a voice which started out strong and brave but which broke under him like thin ice, "I give you thanks, God ... for good neighbors like Johnny Lundeen."

I turned around and looked at Johnny's brother and his wife, who sat a couple of pews behind us. Their eyes were wide open – as if someone had plunged a pin into their rear ends, shocked that Johnny's name had been mentioned out loud in worship. Everyone in that church knew Johnny, or at least knew of him, but few spoke openly about him, especially in church, and few thought of him with gratitude in their hearts. After worship, the men crowded around Pa in order to find out how and why Johnny had suddenly become such a good neighbor, and Pa told them.

After church, Ma drove off with Aunt Vivian to a women's luncheon at the Moravian Church in Ephraim, and Pa brought me home. "Let's check on Johnny before we fix lunch," Pa said.

As we walked toward Johnny's cabin, Pa said, "No chimney smoke. Maybe he's not home."

When we got near the cabin, Champ heard us and began to bark. Pa knocked on the door, which drove Champ crazy. No Johnny. Something wasn't right.

We walked to the nearest window and saw Johnny lying in his bed. Without saying a word, Pa picked up a heavy stick as long as his leg, opened the door, and walked into the cabin. He pointed the stick at Champ and yelled "Get back!" The dog tucked its tail, whined, turned away, and curled up in a cabin corner like a scolded puppy.

Pa hurried to Johnny's bed, and I followed him. What we found was not good. Johnny's hair was as wet as when he'd come up from the bottom of the pond, and his wide white face glistened with sweat. His body shivered so violently that the whole bed shook, and the blanket over him was stained with sweat. Pa laid the palm of his hand across Johnny's forehead and said, "He's burning up! Donna – find a cloth and soak it in cold water."

I looked around the cabin. No cloth. No faucet or water. But I found Johnny's long brown scarf and ran outside, down to the pond. Falling to my belly on the ice, I crawled to the edge of the hole where he and I had broken through, wrapped the scarf around my forearm, and plunged my arm through the thin sheet of new ice.

Back in Johnny's cabin, I unwrapped the dripping scarf from my forearm, and Pa folded it and placed it on Johnny's forehead. The huge man moaned with relief, but the moan triggered a cough so deep and raw that I expected his soft pink guts to come out of his mouth.

"I got to get Doc Vorquist," Pa said. "Can you stay with Johnny?"

I glanced at Champ, still curled in the corner, and nodded.

"That's my girl! I'll be back soon." He gave me the stick and left.

I closed the cabin door and put a handful of finely split maple on top of a single glowing log in the stove. Champ and I hardly took our eyes off one another until Johnny said, weakly, "Water." I walked alongside his bed, and he opened his eyes. "Miss Donna," he said, happily.

"Where can I get some water?" I asked.

He pulled his arm from under the blanket, lifted his trembling pink and white hand, and pointed to a bottoms-up bucket on the counter below the window. "Under there," he said.

I walked to the counter and lifted the wooden bucket. Under

it: a hand pump, pan, and quart pickle jar. I filled the jar with ice-cold water and took it to him. He licked his lips like a dog about to get a treat and took the jar with his badly shaking hands, spilling water over his blanket and chest before he got the jar to his lips, downing the water that was left in a few gulps.

Holding the jar up to me, he nodded for more, and half-spilled, half-guzzled five more jars of water, followed by a fit of dry, raw coughing which sounded so much like a barking dog that Champ lifted his head and eyed his master.

After Johnny stopped coughing and got his breath, he said, "I guess I'm pretty sick."

Tears came to my eyes, and I put my hands up to hide them. A moment later, his hand gently pulled my hands away from my face. It was the first time he had touched me.

"What's wrong, Miss Donna?" he asked.

My lips trembled, and I looked at the floor. "If I hadn't fallen through the ice, you wouldn't be sick."

He thought for a moment and said, "If I hadn't fallen through the ice, you wouldn't be visiting me."

Startled by his kindness, I looked up at him and said, "Pa went to get Doc Vorquist."

Johnny nodded, closed his eyes, and rested.

I pulled up a chair and put my hands on the bed to keep it from shaking so much and closed my eyes too, hoping that I could pray, but still only able to think of going down in the pond. Something wet pressed against my hand, and I jumped. Champ had left the corner, was sitting alongside my chair, and had touched my hand with his nose. He turned from me to his master and laid his head across the edge of the bed.

An hour later, Pa returned with Doc Vorquist and Ma, and their arrival woke up Johnny and sent Champ back into the corner. Doc, a thin, silver-haired man, set his black leather bag on the bed, took off his coat, and said to Johnny, "I see you have a good nurse."

Johnny, no longer shivering, looked at me and said, "The best!" Again, he began coughing.

Doc Vorquist listened to the cough, and when it ended, said, "That's a nasty cough, Mr. Lundeen. But it's a dry cough – that's good." Doc Vorquist opened his bag, took out a thermometer, shook down the silver mercury, and slid it between Johnny's lips. Next, he plugged the ends of his stethoscope into his ears, bent over the bed, and laid the steel amplifier against Johnny's chest, tilting his head, listening. He pulled back and said, "You do have a little fluid in your lungs. Have you been able to cough up any?"

Johnny shook his head.

Doc took the thermometer out of Johnny's mouth, held it up to the light coming through the window. "One hundred three," he said. "You have a stiff fever, Mr. Lundeen. A fever is caused by an infection. I'm going to give you a shot of penicillin, which will help your body fight the infection."

While Doc prepared and loaded his syringe, Ma rolled Johnny onto his side and unbuttoned the rear vent of his red union-suit, revealing Johnny's pale, hairy butt. I looked away.

After the shot, Doc said, "Mr. Lundeen, you need penicillin every three hours, day and night, for at least three days. I can check on you each day, but you'll need someone who can stay with you and give you the injections."

Johnny blinked and shrugged his shoulders.

"What about your brother?" Doc asked.

Johnny shook his head.

"His brother won't have a thing to do with him," Pa said.

"I'll nurse him," Ma said.

"I'll show you how to draw a syringe and give an injection," Doc said. "And I'll give you aspirin to bring down his fever." He turned back to Johnny and said, "With any luck, Mr. Lundeen, we'll have you back on your feet in a few days. But in the meanwhile, you stay in bed, stay warm, drink lots of fluids, and let yourself be nursed. You understand?"

Johnny nodded and closed his eyes.

Ma sat with Johnny the rest of the afternoon, while Pa and I went home, did the chores, and made soup and biscuits. We packed the dinner and walked over to Johnny's. Dad quietly knocked on Johnny's door, and Ma let us in. We glanced at Johnny. He was shivering again and did not look good. Ma said, "He's no better, maybe a little worse." Champ smelled the hot soup and biscuits and began to whine, so I put a biscuit on the floor in front of him while Mom slipped big spoonfuls of soup between Johnny's lips. After this, Ma turned to me and said, "Your father will spend the night here. You and I will go home and check back in the morning."

Alongside the pond, I asked Ma, "Will Johnny be alright?"

Trying to calm me, she put her arm around me and said, "Most sickness gets worse by night, better by day."

"Why won't Johnny's brother help take care of him?"

After considering her answer, she said, "I guess he's afraid of Johnny, like you used to be."

"Why is he afraid of him?"

She paused and said, "Johnny got rough with Emma."

Back in my bedroom, I turned out the lights and looked across the pond to Johnny's cabin. Smoke came out of the chimney, but no fiddle played. A full moon, cold and white against the black sky, reflected off the pond ice. My body let loose with a shiver from head to toe, and I leapt back in bed.

The next morning, Ma and I made a big breakfast, filled the basket, and walked down the hill and past the pond, stopping in our tracks when we heard Johnny cough. His cough was different, no longer dry and rasping but gurgling and bubbling, as if a pool of pond water remained at the bottom of each lung.

Pa, his face drawn and tired, met us at Johnny's door and said, "He's worse yet."

Alarmed, Ma asked, "Have you been giving him his shots?"

Irritated, Pa said, "Of course, woman! What do you take me for? Them shots ain't doing him any good. I'm going to get Doc Vorquist right now, find out if there's anything else we can do for him."

I got Johnny to drink a glass of apple juice and fed Champ the fried eggs and bacon which Johnny refused to eat. Johnny breathed through his mouth, and as his chest rose and fell, his lungs gurgled and wheezed. Each time he tried to speak to me, he began coughing, and after each cough, he spit globs of brown sticky mucus into a bowl by his side.

Pa had trouble finding Doc Vorquist, who was out and about, visiting patients. He finally caught up with him at Frances Elderberry's, the doctor's fingers pressed into her soft stomach, assessing her tumor.

Pa brought Vorquist back with him, and the doctor examined

Johnny for a second time, saying nothing until he finished. "I don't understand it. The penicillin should be working, but the infection is worse, much worse." Puzzling out loud over what to do next, he said, "We could take him to the hospital in Sturgeon Bay, but I don't think they could do much more for him there, and moving him now would not be good."

Johnny raised his head off his pillow and startled all of us by shouting, "No hospital!" He flared his eyes, closed his mouth, and dropped his head back to the pillow, exhausted.

"What more can we do for him here?" Ma asked.

Doc Vorquist thought a long time before answering. "Well, he's an awful big man – three hundred pounds, maybe more. His dose may not be enough. Keep the three-hour schedule, but increase the dose – half again as much." He showed Ma and Pa the increased amount to be drawn with each syringe and said, "Let's hope this helps. I'll be back tomorrow."

Pa and I went home. He walked into the front room, dropped into his favorite arm chair, and fell sound asleep, his head back, his mouth open, exhausted from his night vigil. I fed and brushed Lady, cleaned out her stall, and warmed a pot of soup for dinner. The aroma of tomatoes, onions, meat, and beans simmering on the stove woke Pa. We ate in silence.

After dinner, Pa made a few phone calls – including one to Johnny's brother, Gustav, which did not go well, and ended with Dad saying: "*Accch!* We're doing nursing you should be doing!"

Pa and I packed a dinner and went back to Johnny, who did not open his eyes. His chest rattled with each breath. I fed Champ and returned home with Ma.

Ma and I got up at dawn, Christmas Eve day. We made half a

dozen pancakes the size of dinner plates, packed them up, and went to Johnny's. I knocked quietly on the door and Pa came outside, closing the door behind him, his face drawn and serious, holding a leather bag of Johnny's tools.

"How is he?" I asked, alarmed.

Pa shook his head, which made me think that Johnny had died during the night, and my heart came up my throat, but Pa added, "He had a bad night – sweats and crazy talk, but now he's quiet and awake." Pa took me by the arms, and said, gently, "He wants to see you, alone. Think you can do that?"

Pa opened the door, and I walked to Johnny's bedside. He lay still and quiet, his hands folded across his chest as if arranged by an undertaker. He is dead! I thought, frightened, but he opened his eyes, blinked his crusty eyelids, and said, "Miss Donna."

"Hello, Johnny."

"Look under my bed."

I dropped to my knees.

"What do you see?" he asked.

The ropes and mattress sagged under his weight, almost touching the cover of a beat-up leather case. "A suitcase," I said.

"Bring it up here and open it."

I set the case on the bed, unlatched three rusty clips, and opened it. The inside held a fiddle and bow, encircled by olive-green velvet.

"If I had more strength, I'd play you a tune."

"You could play a Christmas carol!"

"I don't know none .... Do you?"

I nodded.

"Sing one for me."

His quiet request startled me, but a carol came to mind and in an unsteady voice I sang:

O little town of Bethlehem,
How still we see thee lie;
Above thy deep and dreamless sleep,
The silent stars go by.

Yet in thy dark streets shineth
The everlasting light;
The hopes and fears of all the years
Are met in thee tonight.

Johnny smiled, looked at me and said, "I gave my tools to your Pa. I want you to take my fiddle. You both been good to me."

Shaking my head, I said, "No – you'll play again."

Ignoring my protest, he said, "I asked a favor of your Pa, and I got to ask a favor of you, too."

This time, I did not protest, but waited to hear his request. He lifted his hand and arm and touched a single tear running down my cheek with his pink and white thumb that could fill a beer glass.

"Take Champ home, make him your dog."

Those were Johnny Lundeen's last words on this earth, and he spoke them to me.

The favor he had asked of Pa was to be given a decent send-off and burial, so Pa spent part of Christmas Day arranging things with Reverend Sturdevent, insisting that I be allowed to bring Champ into church for the funeral.

Two days later, Reverend Sturdevent, dressed in his black robe, entered the sanctuary through a small narrow door behind the altar which Johnny could never have made it through. The sanctuary was still decorated with red ribbons and fragrant evergreen branches. The minister walked to the chancel, lifted and spread his arms wide, and said, "The Lord giveth, and the Lord taketh away. Blessed be the name of the Lord."

Ma and I sat in the front pew with Champ curled up by my feet, while Pa and seven other big strong fishermen in dark suits, white shirts, dark ties, and black shoes carried Johnny's seven-foot-long casket up the aisle, past Johnny's cousins, aunts, and uncles, past Gustav and Emma, their two faces stretched tighter than the strings on Johnny's fiddle.